"A shot cracked in the air . . . "

Clint dropped down from Eclipse's back and landed in a crouch with the stallion between himself and the direction of the gunshot. At the same time his feet hit the dirt, Kyle's body dropped face first onto the ground to reveal a small hole in the back of his head.

Keeping his head down low, Clint hurried out from behind his horse, searching the area for any sign of whoever had taken that shot. The street was crowded with people of all ages caught in the middle of their daily routines. As the gunshot echoed in the air, those people scattered in every direction, not giving him the slightest clue as to where he should look.

For a second, Clint swore he could see a small wisp of smoke hovering overhead and dispersing into the slowly moving wind. Although that would have been a direct line between the cloud and Kyle, there was nobody else standing there at the moment. What few people Clint could see were ducking into stores or hurrying away down the street.

"Damn," Clint whispered.

DON'T MISS THESE
ALL-ACTION WESTERN SERIES
FROM THE BERKLEY PUBLISHING GROUP

THE GUNSMITH by J. R. Roberts
Clint Adams was a legend among lawmen, outlaws, and ladies. They called him . . . the Gunsmith.

LONGARM by Tabor Evans
The popular long-running series about U.S. Deputy Marshal Long—his life, his loves, his fight for justice.

SLOCUM by Jake Logan
Today's longest-running action Western. John Slocum rides a deadly trail of hot blood and cold steel.

BUSHWHACKERS by B. J. Lanagan
An action-packed series by the creators of Longarm! The rousing adventures of the most brutal gang of cutthroats ever assembled—Quantrill's Raiders.

DIAMONDBACK by Guy Brewer
Dex Yancy is Diamondback, a Southern gentleman turned con man when his brother cheats him out of the family fortune. Ladies love him. Gamblers hate him. But nobody pulls one over on Dex . . .

WILDGUN by Jack Hanson
Will Barlow's continuing search for his daughter, kidnapped by the Blackfeet Indians who slaughtered the rest of his family.

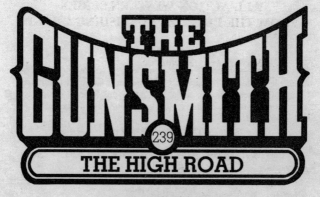

THE GUNSMITH

239

THE HIGH ROAD

J. R. ROBERTS

J

JOVE BOOKS, NEW YORK

This is a work of fiction. Names, characters, places, and incidents are either the product of the author's imagination or are used fictitiously, and any resemblance to actual persons, living or dead, business establishments, events, or locales is entirely coincidental.

THE HIGH ROAD

A Jove Book / published by arrangement with the author

PRINTING HISTORY
Jove edition / November 2001

Visit our website at www.penguinputnam.com

ISBN: 0-515-13185-7

A JOVE BOOK®
Jove Books are published by The Berkley Publishing Group,
a division of Penguin Putnam Inc.,
375 Hudson Street, New York, New York 10014.
JOVE and the "J" design
are trademarks belonging to Penguin Putnam Inc.

PRINTED IN THE UNITED STATES OF AMERICA

10 9 8 7 6 5 4 3 2 1

ONE

Clint couldn't have been more ready for the onset of spring. It felt as though he'd been riding in the cold weather forever and even Eclipse had begun to lose some of the speed in his steps. The winter had seemed to drag on for years and every time a day came along that didn't freeze the breath in the lungs, both man and horse were grateful for it.

Clint had been heading south for weeks, trying to get himself into a warmer climate, but every time he was nearly out of the cold northern territories, something came up to drag his carcass back into the snow. Whether it was a man who needed help or a woman he couldn't refuse, there was always something to drag Clint away from his chosen path. The only thing that had gone his way lately was winning over three thousand dollars in a poker game that had lasted for three days straight.

This time, he was determined to make it to Santa Fe. Although that wasn't his first choice for a vacation spot, the town did have its benefits, the biggest of which was the hot desert sun. Clint had been to New Mexico more times than he could count and the heat had been stifling and oppressive. Compared to riding slowly over a frozen trail skirting the Rockies, however, that stifling oppressive heat was starting to sound awful good.

The closest he'd come to a warm day had been a few weeks ago when he'd actually made it into southern Utah. But, as always, an urgent matter found its way to him and he was dragged all the way back into Wyoming where the cold had been so drastic that Clint had actually had time to get used to his toes and fingers going numb.

He liked his fair share of winter. Sometimes there wasn't anything prettier than waking up to see big, crystalline snowflakes tumbling from the sky to snag in tree branches covered with shimmering coats of ice. He would be the first one to call a breeze brisk rather than cold. After all, winter was the only time to truly appreciate a steaming hot bowl of soup next to a roaring fire.

Clint liked winter. But riding out in the middle of it for weeks . . . now months . . . on end was definitely not his idea of a good time.

The Rocky Mountains were off to his right, standing tall and pristine in the glaring rays of the sun that reflected off the foot of snow that had fallen over the last two days. With Christmas over, the layers of packed white dust had lost their holiday beauty just as the breeze had gone from brisk to cold . . . damn cold.

He'd just ridden into Colorado the day before and was anxious for the feel of warmth on his back and desert sand in his boots. Perhaps it was the fact that he never seemed to be able to take his gun belt off without some strutting punk taking a shot at him that etched the scowl onto his face. Or perhaps it was the fact that he just never seemed to get to do what he wanted to do.

Feeling his mood slowly changing from bad to worse, Clint shifted in the saddle and laid the reins across Eclipse's back. He clapped his gloved hands and rubbed them together vigorously until the feeling crept back into the tips of his fingers. Using one hand to shield his eyes, Clint twisted around to look at the range of mountains, listening to the way the wind howled around his ears.

The sight was enough to take his breath away.

Looking at the majestic formations of rock, ice and

snow, Clint wondered how he could have felt anything but awe while riding so close to something so grand. The base of the range was covered with blankets of pure white snow and dotted with massive pines. Some of the peaks couldn't even be seen through the clouds amassing up near the top. Every so often, the sun found a frozen river to reflect off of, making the vein of ice look like a shimmering golden path leading up to the heavens.

Suddenly, Clint felt foolish for having ridden so far with his head down and his eyes fixed on the back of Eclipse's neck.

He brought the Darley Arabian stallion to a stop and swung down out of the saddle. Without fully meaning to, Clint began walking toward the mountains at a slow, ambling pace. The snow crunched beneath his heels and blew up into his face. Frozen blades of grass snapped easily in his footprints and his breath curled up from his nostrils. Clint stopped and stared at the mountains for a few minutes and then headed back to Eclipse.

The break was all he needed to make him feel energized enough to continue on without dreading every step. So far, the trail seemed to be all but deserted and there was not another rider in sight. If his luck held out, he wouldn't see anyone until reaching the next town, which was only a few more miles down the road.

Clint moved as though he was afraid to make a sound. In some part of his brain, he was certain that if he made too much noise that someone would come out of nowhere and drag him into another dangerous crisis. For anybody else, the feeling would have been needless paranoia. For Clint Adams, it was almost sensible and definitely understandable.

Careful not to be too loud as he climbed back into the saddle, Clint flicked the reins and got Eclipse moving once again just as a gentle snow began to drift down from the clouds that lay scattered across the sky. Already, thoughts of the New Mexico heat began slipping back into his brain as the cold started to gnaw on his bones.

*   *   *

Clint's luck held out all the way to the town of Brookins,
Colorado. He didn't come across another soul or even
hear another voice until he caught sight of a trail of black
smoke creeping up toward the blue sky. After spotting
that first chimney, others made themselves known and
soon he could see movement between the buildings of a
fairly large mining town.

Brookins was a town that had been built at the foot of
the Rockies and shared a history similar to so many of
the other towns in this part of the country. Surely there
was a worked-out vein of gold somewhere in the mountains that still captivated the imaginations of a good
amount of locals. Clint didn't even need to hear the stories
before he knew what they would be about.

More than likely, one of the founding fathers had struck
it rich and some of the others had made enough to move
on to California or even back east. In recent years, the
gold had probably thinned out, leaving behind a town and
a lot of hopeful families waiting for the next big strike.

Thinking this, Clint felt like a jaded old-timer who'd
been around for too long. He shook his head and touched
his heels to Eclipse's side, wondering how long ago he'd
let himself become so crusty around the edges.

Too much time in the cold, he knew. That was all. After
a nice hot meal in front of a big fire, he'd be back to his
former self. A hot bath and a night in a soft bed wouldn't
hurt too much either.

By the time he rode up to the town's livery, he was
ready to spend the rest of the day inside a nice hotel. But
then something caught his attention. It was a sudden
sound that caused both Clint and Eclipse to turn their
heads in search of the source. The sound was something
familiar to them both, although neither had been expecting
it.

It was cheering, followed by a round of enthusiastic
applause.

Having been raised in the circus of P. T. Barnum,

Eclipse was no stranger to applause. And though Clint wasn't quite from the same type of background, the raucous noise was quite unmistakable. But with no tents, brightly colored wagons, or even garishly decorated posters to be seen, Clint knew there was probably no circus in town.

"What's going on over there?" Clint asked the liveryman after handing over Eclipse's reins.

At first, the slim young man with the handlebar mustache looked confused. Then, when another wave of clapping filtered down the street, he nodded. "Oh that? That'd be the fights, mister. We've been having 'em all week since Rory Calhoun came into town."

"Is he any good?"

"Hell, he's the champ. We've got some roughnecks in these parts that've come by to take their chances. Makes for some damn fine shows."

Clint couldn't think of the last time he'd seen a good boxing match. With nothing else to do for the rest of the night, the fights didn't seem like too bad of an idea. "I didn't miss too much, did I?" he asked.

The liveryman shook his head. "Nah. They just got started. Calhoun probably ain't even suited up yet. They'll be working their way through the undercard for another hour or two. You gonna be heading that way?"

"Actually," Clint said, "I just might."

TWO

Finding where the fight was being held was as simple as tracking down the noise, which seemed to flood down the streets. As he made his way through the town, Clint passed a variety of hotels and saloons that seemed all but empty at the moment. Judging by the loud cheers and boos coming from the next street over, nearly all the residents of Brookins were watching the fight.

Clint stepped into a modest-looking hotel along the way where he booked a room and dropped off his gear. From there, he hurried over to a large building situated behind a stretch of brothels on Jones Avenue. As he got closer, Clint was nearly bowled over by the sound of screaming voices, soon to be followed by a clanging bell. Just as that died down, he was inside the building.

"Got a ticket?" a man asked. He was wearing a battered derby and suspenders over a gray shirt. His pants were streaked with black grease and his boots looked as though they'd been around twice as long as the rest of him.

Straining to get a look behind the man, Clint shook his head. "How much?"

"Two bits."

Clint handed over the money and stepped past the man. The inside of the building was so warm, it reminded him of the summertime humidity that he'd been missing for so long. The main difference was that a summer breeze didn't stink of the body odor of no less than fifty screaming miners.

Between the spectators and a crude ring made up of ropes strung around four large barrels, every inch of space in the large room was filled. Sawdust crunched beneath Clint's boots as he shoved his way through the crowd. By the time he got within sight of the ring, a fresh pair of fighters was making their way to their corners.

The man who'd given Clint his ticket stepped inside the ring to announce the fighters, but the crowd was too noisy for Clint to make out anything but the occasional word or two. Since he didn't recognize either of the combatants anyway, Clint didn't worry about the announcer's words and instead waited for the fight to begin.

As soon as the man in suspenders stepped between the ropes, a bell clanged loudly and both of the fighters stalked forward. Neither of the men were very big, but their muscles were like knotted ropes beneath their skin. It was plain by the crooked noses on their faces and the scars on their hands that this was neither man's first time inside the ring.

They stepped forward slowly, bobbing their heads from side to side once they got within arm's reach of each other. Both of them wore dirty pants that looked like they'd been pieced together from oily rags. The bigger of the two had hair so thick on his chest and back that he probably wouldn't even be too cold if he stepped outside. The second was younger and leaner, and couldn't keep the fear from showing in his eyes.

The younger fighter looked even more inexperienced when he took his first swing. Even from where he was standing, Clint could see the kid's hand shaking as it was thrown out toward the older man's jaw. The blow connected, but only hard enough to get his opponent's attention and snap his head slightly back.

Even so, the crowd erupted at the punch as though it was a knockout blow. Clint couldn't help but get wrapped up in the moment and could feel a cheer forming in his throat. A smile crept onto his face and he leaned forward, eager for the match to start in earnest.

Not wanting to let the kid get in too many punches too quickly, the older fighter hopped back on his heels and then lunged forward with a stiff jab that caught the kid right on the nose. That brought the crowd to a frenzy, which only got worse when a solid left hook came around to knock the kid onto his ass.

He didn't know why, but Clint found himself rooting for the younger boxer. "Come on," he called out with the crowd. "Get up! You've got more than that!"

The kid couldn't have heard Clint, but he shook his head and struggled to get back to his feet. He seemed a bit less tentative this time, and was the first one to swing after closing the distance between them. His first was steadier and a bit quicker, which allowed him to catch the older man in the ribs. He followed up with a right uppercut to the stomach and another left hook to the eye.

That staggered the older man, causing him to step back and press up against the ropes. As soon as the kid came in again, the older fighter grinned slightly and brought his arms in close to his body. What followed was a devastating combination of rights and lefts that landed on the kid's face and gut in a hailstorm of bloody knuckles. Blood flowed from the kid's nose and mouth, ran down his face, and fell in drops onto the dirty wooden floor.

By this time, Clint and the entire crowd were whooping and hollering, which added fuel to the fire behind the older man's fists. The more experienced fighter forced the kid all the way across the ring until the ropes and the men in the front row were the only things keeping the guy on his feet. The final blow came like it had been shot from a cannon and dropped the kid into an unconscious heap on the floor.

The man in suspenders gave a ten-count before lifting the older man's hand in victory. Clint's view was completely blocked by the cheering crowd who now huddled in small groups to pass wagered money between themselves. By the time Clint could see the ring again, the kid was being helped to his feet by a blonde woman dressed in a long wool coat and a boy who did his best not to get trampled amid all the excitement.

Reaching up to feel his brow, Clint found that he was sweating. After an entire season of being chilled to the bone, Clint was finally in a place where he didn't feel as though he would freeze to the ground if he stayed still for a few minutes. Of course, staying still in this crowd would have been a trick in itself.

"Bet, mister?" came a voice from Clint's left.

Turning as best he could in the cramped quarters, Clint found the man in suspenders looking at him expectantly.

"Excuse me?" Clint asked.

"I asked if you wanted to place a bet. Got two more fights and then the main event. Now's the time to wager if you wanna beat the rush."

"Who's fighting Calhoun?"

"Some pug named Rayburn. Local kid who's been making a name for himself over the last year or so. Y'ask me, I'd say he ain't got a shot."

"Not a very good way to support local talent."

The man in suspenders shrugged and nodded to another eager gambler vying for his attention. "It ain't my business to support. I take the money and set the odds. Calhoun's favored three to two."

"Then put my money on the pug," Clint said while handing over a half-dollar. "Nobody ever got rich quick by betting on the favorites."

"Suit yerself."

Clint's money was taken and he was given a slip of paper with a mark scribbled in pencil on one side. The man in suspenders was swallowed up by the crowd in a matter of seconds and Clint managed to take advantage of the commotion to get closer to the ring. He didn't know this Rayburn from a hole in the ground, but still bet on the long shot just to spice up his evening.

When he saw the contender enter the ring after the next two matches, Clint thought his bet might not have been such a bad one after all. That feeling lasted all of two minutes . . . which was exactly how long it took for Calhoun to make his way through the mob and step between the ropes.

THREE

If a man could have been constructed out of bricks, mortar and iron plates, that man would have been Rory Calhoun. Standing six feet three inches and weighing in at no less than three hundred pounds, Calhoun was the human equivalent of the mountains looking down on the town itself.

His chest was a solid mass of muscle covered with thick matted hair that would have looked more appropriate on a bear's hide. His legs were stout tree trunks as were his arms. There wasn't a single bristle of hair on his scalp, however, which was a stark contrast to the bushy beard sprouting from his chin. When he stepped inside the ring, he raised his hands as though the fight was already won, grinning to the wild ovations of the rambunctious crowd.

Standing in the opposite corner, Ed Rayburn shifted from one foot to another and cracked his knuckles. Standing just over six feet tall, Rayburn had the look of a man who'd spent his entire life hacking out an existence in the wilds. His hands were covered with calluses gained from years of shoveling coal into steam engines and swinging an ax amid blizzards. His frame was noticeably leaner than Calhoun's, but that was only because it would have taken a freak of nature to be bigger than the reigning champion. Slowly turning his head from side to side, Ray-

11

burn focused on the cracking of his bones rather than the
bloodthirsty audience and tried to think about nothing besides the years of hard work that had brought him to this
point.

There weren't a lot of men tough enough to make a
living in the fighting business. In fact, working some of
the deepest mines in the region was safer than climbing
into that ring. But Rayburn was tougher than most men.
All that remained to be seen was whether or not he was
tougher than Rory Calhoun.

The bell clanged twice and Calhoun swung his hands
out to either side in an effort to work out some of the
cramps given to his muscles by the cold. The fight was
on, but neither man was in any hurry to start. Calhoun
knew it was always better to milk a crowd and Rayburn
was enjoying the last pain-free moments he'd be feeling
for a good long time.

Both big men circled each other a few times, sizing up
one another and getting a feel for the ring. The floorboards
were cold and uneven beneath their feet and the ropes had
been loosened from the previous bouts of the night. Rayburn knew better than to throw the first punch since that
was how Calhoun's last three opponents had started their
matches.

Someone in the crowd next to Clint leaned forward and
smacked his fist on top of one of the barrels making up
the corner of the ring. "Come on already!" he screamed.
"Just kill 'im and be done with it!"

With that, the rest of the crowd began shouting for
blood. It wasn't long before the champ moved in to deliver it to them.

Calhoun's lip turned up in an animal snarl as his arm
shot out toward Rayburn's face. The fist at the end of that
arm was the size of a ham hock and even though the
contender slid to the side, Calhoun still managed to clip
the side of Rayburn's chin. For a glancing blow, the
punch got enough reaction to make someone think the
fight was over.

Clint had gotten a good look at the challenger, however, and knew this fight had just begun.

Blinking away the effects of the shot he'd taken, Rayburn moved around to the champ's side and sent out a quick jab to Calhoun's solid midsection. His fist might just as well have slammed against a side of beef for all the damage it did, but it had its desired effect. Rayburn waited for the bigger man to look in his direction, and followed up with a solid punch to Calhoun's face.

The champ's ribs hadn't been the same since a match he'd had in New York City two years ago. The bout had made it into the papers as did his injury and when another fighter purposely hit him in that spot, Calhoun always saw red. It made his next few breaths painful and reminded him of the beating he'd taken those years earlier. But more than that, it pissed him off. Everyone knew how much he hated when someone snuck a punch into that trick rib.

If there was one thing that every fighter knew, it was not to get mad while in the ring. Sure, a little bit of rage was good for the amateurs or in a street fight. But if you wanted to have any kind of stamina, anger was not the way to get it. When Rayburn sunk that punch into Calhoun's sore rib, he knew the champ was on the edge of snapping. When he sunk in the second shot, he pushed the champ completely over.

The tricky part, he knew, would be to stay out of the way until Calhoun burned himself out. On the other hand, if he got caught by any of those first few shots, Rayburn could pretty much say goodbye to his face as he knew it.

Calhoun charged in with a deadly scowl etched onto his face. His right hand tore through the air, aimed at Rayburn's skull, coming in like a runaway train. He knew he landed something when he felt his first impact on bone. That shot spun the contender in a half-circle, setting him up for another punch coming in right behind the first. All of Calhoun's weight went into the follow-up and when it missed, it sent his entire body stumbling forward.

With his brain still rattled by the blow that had clipped his jaw, Rayburn felt half of his body go numb. He managed to focus in on the other half and was just able to step aside before getting decapitated by the champ's second shot. As Calhoun's momentum forced him to take a shaky step forward, Rayburn cocked his arm back like a piston and drove a fist straight into the champ's nose.

Rayburn could feel cartilage breaking and knew he'd struck pay dirt. From the corner of his eye, he could see the man in suspenders practically diving for the hammer so he could end the round. But before he heard the familiar clang, Rayburn twisted his body and put all of his weight behind one last blow into Calhoun's stomach.

The champ nearly folded around Rayburn's fist and all the air came rushing from his lungs in a painful wheeze. The bell sounded just as Calhoun hit the floor and it was obvious that he wasn't getting up anytime soon.

No matter how hard Calhoun's manager and the man in suspenders tried to revive him, the champ couldn't even sit up on his own. By now, the crowd was screaming at the top of their lungs and every bet collector in the place was being stampeded by the few anxious gamblers who'd put their money on a long shot.

Clint kept his eyes on the fighters, however, watching as that same blonde woman and little boy came out to help Rayburn out of the ring. This time, the woman seemed more concerned with the man's health and the little boy could barely keep himself from jumping excitedly up and down.

Once Calhoun was back on his feet and being helped from the ring, Clint tapped the man with suspenders on the shoulder. "I think you owe me some money."

FOUR

The first thing Clint noticed once the commotion had worn down was that the champ and his manager did not look at all happy. Although they shouldn't have been too pleased with losing a fight, they seemed as though they were more than just upset with a bad night. They were looking for payback. They were looking for blood.

The next thing Clint noticed was that Rayburn, the blonde woman, and the kid were nowhere to be found.

Rather than say anything to the man in suspenders, even though he seemed to be the one who knew all there was to know about the fighters, Clint stepped outside and flagged down one of the locals. He made sure to pick one who looked happy with the turnout.

"Excuse me," Clint said to a man who wore a smile that stretched from ear to ear. "You got the time?"

The man gazed up at the stars and stuck his hands deeper inside his pockets. "Got to be closing in on eight o'clock. I ain't got a watch, though."

"I don't know about you, but I can afford to buy a watch after this fight," Clint said with a knowing wink.

"You bet on Eddie, too?"

"If you're talking about the man who put Calhoun in his place, then yeah. I sure did bet on Eddie."

Now the other man seemed to relax a bit. "I talked to

15

Eddie night before last. He said he was gonna win this fight tonight if it killed him."

"By the look in Calhoun's eye after that first punch, I'd say it nearly did just that."

"I reckon you're right, stranger."

"Where is Eddie, anyway? I'd like to buy him a drink to celebrate tonight's victory."

A brisk wind had begun to tear down the street, raking through both men's skin and gnawing into their bones. The other man pulled the collar of his coat up around his ears and hooked his head in the direction of the saloon district. "If'n he's in the mood for a drink, he'd be at Sal's just down the street. But he might'a just gone home, seein' as how much trouble he's in."

"Trouble?"

"Calhoun don't like to lose. I heard he found the last guy that beat him after the fight. Some poor joker in Prescott. Beat him half to death in an alley."

"Not very sportsmanlike."

The other man simply shrugged. "Not a very nice sport. It's gettin' colder, so's I'll be headin' off. If you catch up with him, buy Eddie a drink for me."

Clint waved as the other man turned and headed off down the street. "Will do."

There was no more cheering and no more clanging bells or raucous laughter floating down the street. The only sound Clint could hear was the occasional foot crunching on snow and the cold wind howling between darkened buildings. As he headed in the direction of Sal's, Clint could once again hear voices. This time, they sounded more like what he would expect from a lot of folks gathered in one place and not some half-crazed mob.

Clint had walked half a block, and noticed that the crowds from the fight had moved around to the gambling parlors and bordellos, searching for a somewhat less bloody form of entertainment. The gaming district went for a solid block in either direction. Like most mining towns, Brookins had apparently put a lot of its energy into keeping the prospectors happy and was prospering off of whatever money those men had managed to pull out of the mountains.

To the left of where Clint was standing, he saw a row of Faro houses and bordellos that appeared to be getting more business than they knew what to do with. To his right were saloons and poker parlors, which also were in no danger of closing early. Clint headed for the saloons and kept his eye open for any familiar faces. When he saw the boy from the fights sitting outside a place on the corner, Clint looked at the letters written across a large picture window.

Sure enough, it was Sal's.

It didn't take a mind reader to know what the kid was thinking. Sitting on the boardwalk with his chin resting on the palms of his hands and a sullen frown on his face, the boy was obviously upset about not being allowed inside the saloon. Before offering his condolences, Clint stepped inside the place and looked for Rayburn. The big fighter was sitting in the middle of a crowd at a table in back.

After ordering a drink, Clint made his way to that part of the room until he was at a table on the outer edge of Rayburn's admirers. It wasn't hard to listen in on what was being said as most of the men near the fighter were loudly congratulating him on his victory whenever possible. The only person who didn't seem pleased was Rayburn himself.

For being a boxer who'd just knocked out the favorite in the first round, Eddie Rayburn looked more like he'd lost everything he held dear. No amount of slaps on his back or free drinks on his table seemed able to lift his spirits. Clint had seen that look before on so many others in his travels. In fact, it was a look that usually led to another one of the detours that he'd been cursing on his way into town. It was the look of someone who knew they were in trouble and Clint thought he had a pretty good idea of what kind of trouble it was.

After a few of the more enthusiastic boxing fans said their good-byes, Clint made his way up to the fighter's table and sat down. He got a few odd looks, but the overall mood in the air was still pretty good. That was, however, until Clint looked over to Rayburn.

The fighter's eyes turned into hard-edged pieces of granite as they turned toward the newest arrival. The muscles in his neck tensed just as he tightened his grip around the mug he'd been holding. When Rayburn spoke, his voice was a low, almost primitive rumble. "Who the hell are you?" the fighter asked.

"Just someone who saw you fight," Clint said. "I was in the front row."

Rayburn's eyes narrowed and he nodded. "Yeah, I saw you. What do you want?"

"Just came over to congratulate you. Maybe buy you a drink. You don't look like you're in much of a celebrating mood, though."

When he looked into Rayburn's eyes, Clint got a taste of what it must have been like to face the other man in the ring. The boxer's face was red and swollen. There was a small cut over his left eye and already bruises were starting to darken his skin. Rayburn glared across the table like a grizzly that was trying to decide which piece to bite off first. Although Clint was no stranger to threatening looks, Rayburn's was one of the best. In fact, before he knew it, Clint's hand was moving away from his beer and closer to his gun.

"I just want to talk, Eddie," Clint said warily.

"Yeah. I'll bet." Rayburn took a moment to sip his drink and then nodded toward the others at his table. "Why don't you fellas give us some privacy. Thanks for coming to see my fight."

"No problem, Eddie," said a small guy in coveralls and a torn coat. "You need any help, you know where to find us."

The laugh that came from Rayburn was more sarcastic

than anything else. "Sure, Mike. I know where to find ya. I think I'll be all right, though."

Mike tried to stare down Clint as well, but his eyes were glazed over and bloodshot. The fact that it took him three tries to get out of his chair didn't do much for his image, either. Finally, the others helped him to his feet and carried him to another table.

"He's drunk," Rayburn said by way of an explanation. "He didn't mean anything."

Clint leaned back in his chair and took his hand away from his gun. "I don't know who you think I am, but you don't have anything to fear from me."

"Oh no? Then why'd Malloy bring you in town?"

"I just got here tonight and nobody sent for me."

"That so?" Rayburn asked while tilting his head to the side. This time, he moved his gaze over Clint in careful inspection. "You got the look of a gunman. I seen plenty of your kind before."

Clint found the edge in his own voice when he answered sternly, "I'm not a gunman." Seeing that he'd put the fighter on his guard again, Clint eased up a bit. "I was just passing through and thought I'd catch the fight. That's all there is to it."

"Then why are you here? If you want to shake my hand, then here it is," Rayburn said while offering a giant, blood-smeared paw. "Thanks for coming and have a safe trip back to your hotel."

Clint did shake the man's hand with a firm grip, but didn't even try to impress Rayburn with any show of strength. The fighter responded in kind, cracking Clint's knuckles even though it was obvious he was holding back.

"You weren't supposed to win tonight, were you?" Clint asked after a moment of silence.

Rayburn's eyes snapped up, gleaming like a wolf's in the dim light of the lanterns hanging on the wall. "What the hell are you sayin', mister?"

"You heard me. I was close enough to see the look on Calhoun's face. He was surprised as hell when you landed

that punch and no fighter becomes champ by getting surprised that easily."

Clint studied Rayburn's face as his words sunk in.
Rather than look offended or angry, the fighter simply
stared down at his drink, swirling the brown liquid around
in its glass.

"And all that money that was changing hands . . . there
was more at that fight than I've seen in some banks," Clint
continued. "That didn't seem like friendly wagering . . .
especially not when you looked at the ones handing out
the cash. When you won, they looked more like they
thought they were being robbed."

"You see an awful lot, don't you?"

"I sure do. Tends to make it easier staying alive that
way. Add all that to the way you got out of there so
quickly and the way you sit here like you're at your own
funeral. It just doesn't add up. Boxing isn't exactly what
anyone would call an honest business, is it?"

"No sir," Rayburn said with a sorrowful shake of his
head. "No, it most definitely is not."

FIVE

"You've got the upper hand, here, mister," Rayburn said. "You seem to know so much, but I don't even know your name."

"It's Clint Adams. And I hope you're not offended by me just coming up and talking to you about all of this, but you looked like a man who might be in over his head. If I'm wrong, just tell me to be on my way."

For the first time since they'd met, Rayburn cracked a smile. "You're not wrong. Just damn peculiar."

"Well, I guess I've gotten some pretty good instincts over the years. More often than not, they seem to pan out for me."

"Since you already seem to know, I guess there's no harm in tellin' you that you were right. I wasn't supposed to win that fight. In fact, this was supposed to be my last time inside a ring for the rest of my life."

"Calhoun's people fixed the match?"

Rayburn nodded. "Yep, but I don't see why. He's a helluva fighter."

"So are you."

"Not so's anyone else would know it. I've been working on my winning record for years now and I still can't pay for a decent roof over my family's heads. Then I finally get a shot at someone like Calhoun and the first thing I hear is that I gotta throw it away . . . right along with my pride and reputation . . . all for a fraction of the champ's cut of the purse."

"The only thing I don't understand is why a great fighter like Calhoun would need to fix his matches when—"

Clint was cut off by the sound of the front door to the saloon slamming open and a set of footsteps hurrying inside. When he turned to look at who'd barged in, Clint saw the kid from the fight who'd also been the same one moping outside all by himself.

"Danny?" Rayburn said in a concerned voice. "What's the matter?"

All the boy could get out was the beginning of a sentence before the front door flew open once again. This time, two men stalked in from the cold. They wore long dark coats and scarves wrapped around their faces. Each carried a double-barreled shotgun in the crook of their elbows.

Danny didn't need to say another word. Just by the way he nervously looked from the two men and then back at Rayburn, it was obvious that they were the reason he'd burst inside. Since he couldn't think of anything else to say, the boy rushed across the room and hid himself behind the massive frame of Ed Rayburn.

Everyone else in the saloon had stopped what they were doing to get a look at the two armed men who'd interrupted their drinking. The bartender, a squat old man with a cauliflower ear, waddled up to them with his hands on his hips. "I don't take too kindly to no one comin' into my place waving their guns around," he said. "Hand 'em over and I'll get yer first drink on the house."

Only one of the dark-clad figures bothered to look over at the old man. His eyes shifted slowly between hat and scarf until they were glaring menacingly at the barkeep. When the old man held out his hands to take the shotguns, the masked newcomer jabbed the butt of his shotgun into his belly.

The barkeep doubled over and hacked out a few breaths. As soon as a few of the patrons got up to move toward the gunners, both men pointed their weapons at the crowd.

"Do you know those men?" Clint asked in a voice only Rayburn could hear.

The fighter shooed the boy away from him until Danny was running for the back door. Only when the kid was out of sight did Rayburn shake his head. "Nope, but I was afraid someone like them was comin'."

The old man took in a shaky breath and slowly raised back up to his full height. As soon as he looked over to the man who'd knocked the air out of his lungs, the same shotgun cracked him in the jaw. This time, he fell to the floor.

"Nobody else needs to get hurt in here," said the shotgunner. Pointing toward Clint and Rayburn's table, he added, "Nobody besides him, that is."

SIX

As soon as Clint saw the pair walk into the saloon, he knew it would come down to a moment like this. Whether or not they knew who he was or what he was doing, men like those always seemed to find him no matter where Clint decided to go. Perhaps there was a bar somewhere in the Yukon territories where he could sit and enjoy a few peaceful drinks without being interrupted by some idiot with a gun.

Just to be on the safe side, Clint kept his mouth shut and his head down for the moment.

The first shotgunner wore a black scarf tied around his face and pointed the barrel of his weapon toward Clint. "You," he said. "Get up and clear away from that dead man you got sittin' at yer table."

Clint looked over toward Rayburn. The fighter wasn't doing much of anything besides shaking his head and swirling his beer mug from side to side. Part of Clint's brain told him to do as he was told and walk away. After all, this wasn't his affair anyhow. Rayburn never asked for his help and even now, didn't seem to want it.

Maybe Clint's biggest problem was the fact that he could never help himself from getting involved with other people's problems. If he stayed to himself more often, his life would definitely be a lot quieter. Then again, there would be a lot more good people who'd wind up on the wrong end of a gun if he never got involved. And that was what it all boiled down to.

In the time it took for Clint to push his chair away from the table, he'd already made up his mind. He wasn't about to walk away from this one, no matter how easy it would have been to do just that. Instead, he was going to stick his nose in one more time where nobody had asked him to go. All because Ed Rayburn looked like a man who needed some help in facing his problems . . . especially when those problems were behind a pair of sawed-off scatter guns and masks.

Clint stood and held his hands up loosely at shoulder level. "If you've got a problem with this man, perhaps it would be easier to talk things out."

"Time for talking has come and gone, mister. Now step aside before you catch some of the lead that's about to fly."

Locking eyes with the man closest to him, Clint took a slow step toward the shotguns. He didn't even flinch when both of the gunmen pulled their hammers back and took aim. He stopped so that one of the gunners was aiming at him instead of Rayburn. From the corner of his eye, Clint saw the fighter get to his feet and square his muscular shoulders at the gun pointed his way.

"I thought Malloy was more of a man than this," Rayburn said. "Not much more, but at least big enough to come and do his own talking."

Clint scanned the bar just to make sure that the two with the shotguns were the only ones he needed to worry about. After glancing over both shoulders, he was fairly sure that nobody else was trying to work their way around behind him. Then he looked at Rayburn, who seemed more annoyed than scared by the confrontation.

"So I take it you know these two?" Clint asked.

Rayburn shrugged. "They could be any of Malloy's men. Or they could be new. It don't matter, though, since they're all the same anyway."

The second shotgunner wore a dark blue scarf and he stepped over the crumpled body of the barkeep as he walked up close to the fighter. "You made a big mistake tonight," he said. "An' someone's gotta pay for it."

Clint reached out to put his hand on the masked man's shoulder. With a strong shove, he forced the man back a step and caused the other gunner to step forward and put the barrel of his gun in Clint's face.

"I don't know who you are, stranger," said the man with the black scarf. "But you'd best step back like we told you before, because we ain't gonna tell you again."

From where he was, Clint could smell cold gun oil mixed in with the scent of powder. Still, he looked back down that barrel and fixed the other man's gaze. Without a word, Clint took a step back, the intensity in his eyes forcing the gunman to do the same.

"You boys are already starting to repeat yourselves," Clint said. "Now why don't you at least pull up a chair where we can talk about this?" Holding his hand over his gun, Clint squared off and stared fearlessly at both men. "I may be outnumbered, but I'll bet I can take at least one of you with me before I go. Either of you care to wager on which it'll be?"

At first, the men seemed mildly amused by the threat. But when they took a moment to notice that Clint wasn't backing down in the slightest, the smiles dropped off of their faces. The second gunner turned to look at the man wearing the black scarf. When black nodded once, both men stepped up behind a chair. Black leveled his gun at Clint, while Dark Blue aimed at Rayburn.

"You want to talk so badly, mister," Black said. "Then sit yer ass down and we'll talk."

As soon as Clint and Rayburn were seated, the shotgunners eased themselves down into their chairs. Once that happened, most of the others in the bar took the opportunity to bolt out the door. There were a few, however, who stood back up and moved to the far end of the bar or one of the tables on the other side of the room.

"How much?" Clint asked simply.

Black's eyes narrowed. "How much what?"

"How much money does Rayburn owe you? This is about money, isn't it?"

Nodding almost imperceptibly, Black tilted his head as though he truly didn't know what to make of all this. "Two thousand dollars."

"And how much are you being paid to do this job?"

"Four hundred."

Leaning forward, Clint put on his best poker face and stared Black dead in the eyes. "Tell you what. I'll give you twenty-four hundred dollars if you let this man live and leave his family alone."

"His family's got nothin' to do with—"

"Don't take me for a fool. Men like you and men like the one who hired you would get around to threatening his family sooner or later," Clint said with no small amount of contempt in his voice. "So we'll cut to the heart of the matter and end all of this. Go back to your boss and tell him I'll pay him in full within the week."

"Is that so?" Looking over to his partner, Black snorted under his scarf and his shoulders began to shake with laughter. "And who the hell are you? His guardian angel or somethin'?"

"My name's Clint Adams." The words came out like icy daggers, which cut through both of the shotgunners and cut their laughter off at the quick. "Now get the hell out of here before I put a bullet into both of you faster than you can even think about pulling those triggers."

For a second, the masked men tensed as though they were about to fire. But after another second passed, Black stood up and motioned for Dark Blue to follow.

"You'll hear from us soon," Black growled before turning on his heel and storming out the front door. Dark Blue was right behind him.

It took a good couple of minutes before Rayburn had enough strength to keep his breath steady and his hands from shaking. Without needing to be asked, the barkeep waddled over with a glass of whiskey for each of them and set them on the table. Rayburn downed his with one swallow, but Clint left his where it was.

"That was the damndest thing I ever seen," the barkeep said in a wheezing, gravelly voice. "Hell, that was worth getting knocked in the gut. Who are you, mister?"

Clint looked around and saw that the half a dozen or so townspeople that were still in the saloon were waiting for the answer with baited breath. Rather than try another bluff, Clint let out the breath he'd been holding and came clean. "You heard what I told them."

"I'll be . . ." the barkeep mused. "Your drinks are on the house, Mister Adams. Just wait till I tell the missus."

Clint sighed and closed his eyes. Suddenly, he could feel a weight pressing down on his shoulders as he once again ran headfirst into the very thing he'd been trying to avoid. Rubbing his temples, Clint wondered why he kept doing these things.

"Mister Adams," came the shaky voice of Ed Rayburn. "Thank you. Thank you so much."

That was why.

SEVEN

When the saloon door came crashing in a second time, Clint thought that the two shotgunners had already changed their minds and were coming to collect on their original debt of blood. Instinctively, his hand went for his pistol and his body twisted to give him a clear look at his oncoming targets.

Before he could clear leather, however, Clint saw the surprised look on the faces of the young boy who'd run out of the saloon earlier as well as the blonde woman he'd spotted at the fights. Both of them looked wide-eyed and frozen with fear when they realized how close they'd come to provoking Clint's reaction.

"It's all right," Rayburn said as he quickly got to his feet and put a calming hand on Clint's elbow.

As soon as Clint saw the woman and boy rushing through the doorway, he was able to rein himself in. "Sorry about that," he said with a small wave.

Once the woman saw that she wasn't about to be shot at, she looked toward Rayburn. The fighter waved her in. Almost immediately, the boy ducked under the blonde's arm and dashed across the floor with the speed of a rambunctious puppy.

"I went . . . I went home as fast as I could, Uncle Eddie," the boy said between excited breaths. "Just like

you told me. I told Mom to give me the gun she keeps
over the fireplace, but she wouldn't and I told her to stay
home, but she said—"

"That's fine," Rayburn said as soon as he could get a
word in edgewise. "Actually, I didn't want either one of
you to come back. Next time I tell you to get out of here,
you go home and stay there. No need getting both of you
in trouble."

At the mere mention of trouble, the kid let his head
droop and his eyes turn toward the floor. "Sorry."

By this time, the blonde had made her way across the
saloon and wrapped her arms around Rayburn. She was
just able to get her hands to meet around the man's massive frame. "Don't blame him, Edward," she said. "There
wasn't a chance of me staying home after what Danny
said was going on down here. Are you all right?"

"Sure I'm all right. Thanks to him."

When Rayburn pointed toward Clint, the woman turned
and looked at him as though it was the first time she'd
seen him standing there. The expression on her face reflected her gratitude, but she was reluctant to leave the
fighter's side.

"Then I owe you my thanks as well," she said. "Are
you a friend of my brother's?"

Clint had been watching the entire scene with a fair
amount of interest. The entire time, he hadn't been able
to tear his eyes away from the stunning blonde. Even
though she was bundled up in layers of thick clothing, she
still managed to move with smooth grace. The steps she'd
taken across the saloon had been fluid and elegant, almost
as though she'd floated over the floorboards.

Her skin had a golden hue that was exceptionally rare
to see this deep into the winter months. Her high cheek-
bones gave her the appearance of always being in some
stage of a smile. For the moment, her hazel eyes were
worried and filled with tears, but they were still stunning
in their own right. Clint wanted nothing more at that moment than to try and make her smile again, even though

he doubted she could get any prettier than she was at the moment.

Realizing he'd been staring at her just long enough for the woman to start getting uncomfortable, Clint stepped forward and extended his hand. "I saw you at the fights earlier," he said. "I thought you were Ed's . . ." He stopped himself just short of sticking his boot in his mouth. ". . . I mean . . . you're his sister?"

Now, the woman did smile. Although it was only a slight upward turn of the corners of her mouth, it was more than enough to light up the room. "He's been my brother as far back as I can remember," she said jokingly. "Danny told me there were five men with guns coming in here."

"Actually, there was only two."

"Still, one man with a gun is dangerous enough." Her eyes drifted to the holster at Clint's side. "Whatever you did for my brother . . . I thank you for it. Mister Malloy has been threatening Ed's life for a while now. It was only a matter of time before he actually tried to do something about it. Just like I've been trying to tell my thick-headed excuse for a brother." Without looking away from Clint, she swatted Rayburn with the palm of her hand, causing him to grunt as though he actually felt the woman's blow.

Feeling as though he was finally able to look away from her, Clint shot a glance toward the front door of the saloon and scanned the people inside. For the most part, everyone seemed to be minding their own business. He went over to the front window, peeked outside, and searched the street. There wasn't anyone heading toward the place or even standing in front of it. Still, something in Clint's gut told him that they'd stayed in one place for too long already.

"Not to worry anyone," Clint said after he walked back to Rayburn, his sister, and the boy, "but we should probably be getting out of here just in case those two decide to double back and finish their job after all."

Rayburn nodded and pulled himself out of his sister's protective grasp. "You're right," he said, looking over to the stout barkeep. The other man gave a curt nod in response and pointed toward the rear of the room. "We can duck out through the back door. That is, if you think it's all right."

"That's perfect," Clint said. "But let me scout it out first."

Danny managed to slip away from his mother and dash to the back door before Clint was halfway across the room. His youthful eyes were wide with excitement and his chest puffed out like a bird displaying its bravery. "I can help you, mister. I spotted them two the first time an' I can do it again!"

Clint paused by the door and the knelt down so he could look the boy straight in the eyes. "Tell you what. How about you go with your mother and make sure that nobody tries to sneak up on us from behind?"

"Awww."

"That's just as important as the man out front. You ask any cavalry officer and they'll tell you the same."

That caused the boy's eyes to light back up again and he scurried back to the woman's side.

Clint managed to keep an easy smile on his face until he turned back around and opened the back door. It led out into an alley that was just big enough for one man to walk through at a time and was black as pitch. In reality, it was just as good a spot for an ambush as anyplace else. The only difference was that Clint had already pegged the gunmen as the types who preferred attacking in numbers rather than forcing themselves to come forward single file. Since they couldn't overpower anyone in the cramped confines of the alley, they would probably come at the front of the building if they were going to come back at all.

Clint figured those two shotgunners were probably still explaining things to their boss, but even the slightest bit of uncertainty could cost a lot when there were lives hanging in the balance. Taking one step in the wrong direction could get one or all of them killed, which was why Clint insisted that he be the first one stepping anywhere.

Clint looked over his shoulder and found Rayburn waiting patiently a few feet behind him with his arms draped over the shoulders of his sister and nephew. The sheer mass of the fighter's body was more than enough to shield the woman and boy from any attack that came from the saloon's front door.

Not wanting to keep Rayburn's back to the door any longer, Clint took a step outside and into the darkness.

The moment he stepped out of the saloon, Clint heard footsteps rushing toward him from the other end of the alley. They were quick and close together, closing in on him fast. In one fluid motion, he drew and spun around, ready to put a bullet into whoever thought they were going to jump him from behind.

What he found was empty air and more darkness. When he looked down, he found a rather surprised looking dog that had frozen in its tracks after rushing toward Clint's boots. Clint let out the breath he'd been holding and holstered his gun.

"It's all right," he said while turning back around.

The shotgun barrel waiting for him looked like a pair of close-set eyes staring back from the night. Clint would have drawn his gun again if he thought he was faster than a falling hammer.

"Good choice," came a hoarse, familiar whisper from a man in the black scarf. "It's also your last."

EIGHT

Even though the only light in the alley was whatever filtered down from the moon through the layer of passing clouds, Clint felt as though he could see every nick and smudge on the barrel of that shotgun. Even the fog from his breath against the metal seemed clear as crystal to his searching eyes.

He then heard the voice of a man from inside the saloon . . . the one that had been wearing the dark blue scarf wrapped around his face. After Clint moved his hand away from his gun, he reached inside the door to quickly wave Rayburn and the others back inside.

"Oh, don't you worry about them," the gunman said. "I'll get to them just as soon as I'm through with you."

Since this wasn't the first time Clint had had a gun pointed in his direction, he managed to keep his voice steady as a rock. "What about my offer?"

"You can shove that up yer ass. I got paid to do a job and no man in my business gets anywhere if they don't follow through. And if'n you really are Clint Adams . . . well, that's just all the better."

Perfect, Clint thought. Another punk kid looking to make a name for himself. It seemed as if they'd been falling out of trees lately. Or maybe Clint was just giving off some kind of a scent that attracted them to him like mosquitoes to a bare neck.

"Look, kid," Clint said while slowly moving his hand back to his pistol. "You won't lose any face if you take my offer to your boss. If he gives the order, you can come back for me later. I won't be going anywhere for a while."

Clint could hear the sharp intake of breath and the desperate tension in the shotgunner's voice. "Don't talk to me like I'm some kid . . ."

When the man in the scarf stopped talking, that was when Clint knew there was going to be trouble. He could almost hear the thoughts that were running behind that scarf, could almost feel the anticipation boiling over inside the younger man. Clint knew the gunman's muscles would be twitching right about now and his palms would be itching as sweat began to soak into the shotgun's grip.

Using his instincts as his only guide, Clint waited another half second before ducking down and reaching out with his left hand to grab hold of the shotgun just in front of the trigger guard. The gunpowder exploded with a fiery burst as Clint pushed the barrel up and out of his face. The barrel became instantly hot against his skin, but Clint didn't dare let it go.

From inside the saloon, the blonde woman screamed and Rayburn threw himself over her and the boy. They all hit the floor with a solid *thump* as everyone else inside the bar began to dive behind cover for the second time that evening.

"It's gonna be all right," Rayburn whispered as another explosion sounded from outside. "I won't let anything happen to you."

The shotgun went off a second time as Clint grabbed hold of it with both hands and pulled it from the gunman's grasp. This time, when the heat blazed through Clint's palms, he pitched the gun off to the side and behind him. His ears rang with blaring pain and large red blobs danced in front of his eyes from the flash of gunpowder.

Luckily for him, Clint was close enough to the other man to know where the gunner stood and was able to strike out with his fist even though he couldn't see much more that an afterimage of the blast. His first punch went low and made contact with the younger man's stomach, causing the gunner to cough loudly and stagger backwards. Before he lost contact with him, Clint sent out another quick jab, which bounced off the other man's shoulder.

Suddenly, he could hear another round of gunfire coming from inside the saloon. Before he could worry about that, however, Clint knew he had to finish dealing with the scuffle he'd started.

Clint's vision began to clear after a few quick swipes of his eyes with the back of his hand. The first thing he saw was the outline of the man in the scarf. He could see that the guy had moved back about ten feet. He was pulling his coat to one side and grabbing for something at his hip.

Before he could think twice about it, Clint's hand flashed to his holster and drew his modified Colt. Normally, once he drew, the trigger was as good as pulled. But this time he paused for less than a second . . . just long enough to see the glint of moonlight off the other man's gun. Certain that the gunman was indeed about to fire, Clint squeezed off his own shot and placed a bullet straight through the other man's heart.

Clint had still managed to drop the gunner before the younger man even had the chance to clear leather. He turned and ran back inside the saloon as the corpse fell to the cold ground.

Inside, he caught a glimpse of two figures standing shoulder to shoulder at the front of the room. Both men were dressed in similar knee-length coats with their faces covered by dark scarves. One held a Winchester rifle and the other carried a shotgun. The image of both of them burned into his eyes as they turned to face him. Clint was certain that both of those guns would be belching out clouds of smoke and tongues of flame within the next second.

It was too late for him. Clint knew he'd stepped through that door at just the wrong time and was about to get blown off his feet. When he felt the impact, it hit him like a freight train and sent him through the air.

The only strange thing was that the impact came from the side rather than the front. His body was on fire with a dull pain as he impacted heavily against the floor, but somehow he was still conscious and breathing. When he tried to feel for bloody wounds, he found that he couldn't even move his arms. Couldn't so much as roll onto his back.

He couldn't see.

Everything was black and the sound was a muffled mixture of garbled voices and pounding footsteps.

And then, just as suddenly as it had gone, Clint's sight returned as well as all the noises in the saloon. Rayburn was getting to his feet and bending down to offer a hand. It was then that Clint realized he hadn't been shot at all. Instead, the burly fighter had tackled him from the side just in time to get both of them out of harm's way.

Rather than take the hand being offered to him, Clint rolled to his stomach and thanked the lord above that he'd managed to hold onto his gun this entire time. Both of the masked men were still standing at the front of the saloon, turning for another shot at Clint and Rayburn.

"Get down," Clint shouted over the ringing in his ears.

Once again, his vision was obscured by gun smoke as another round of explosions rocked the saloon.

Some of the lead from the shotgun spread out far enough to tear shallow, painful grooves down Clint's back, but the rifle's round didn't even come close to its mark. The wounds stung, but Clint had gotten deeper scratches from an overenthusiastic lover back in Oregon.

Clint made sure not to waste any more time. His finger squeezed off two rounds in quick succession. The first spun the rifleman around in a tight circle and the second dropped the shotgunner right onto his back. Before either of the two could get a chance to make another move, Clint was on his feet and stalking toward them. He took two steps before the rifleman twisted around with gun in hand and tried to take aim.

Clint's pistol barked once more, carving a tunnel straight through the rifleman's head.

At first, the entire saloon looked empty except for Clint, Rayburn, and the corpses. But once it was obvious that the shooting was over, some shuffling noises came from behind the bar.

"That you, ma'am?" Clint asked as he slowly positioned himself to get a look at who was hiding behind the bar.

For a moment, whoever it was tried to keep quiet and not be noticed. But then the barkeep came shuffling forward amid the tinkling of broken glass and scraping of splintered wood. As soon as he came out into the open, the pudgy man got to his feet and held his hands up high.

"She's back here," he said. "And so's the boy. Is it all clear?"

Rayburn walked past the barkeep and grabbed hold of his sister and nephew. "It looks all right for now. We'd better get out of here while we can."

NINE

"They *what*?"

The man screaming those words did so with an explosion of sound and fury that rocked the armed men back on their heels as though they'd been struck with a shovel. Mister Malloy jumped to his feet and pounded on his desk with two little fists that seemed almost ridiculously small for such a heavy man.

Malloy wasn't tall by any means, but he carried all of his considerable weight right around his midsection in a gut that blossomed out of him like something that was only seconds away from exploding. His face and neck had turned bright red in the space of a few seconds and sweat started pouring down his cheeks. A scraggly ring of brown hair was slicked down onto his skull, resembling lines that had been drawn in with a thin pencil. The squat fingers he jabbed into the air were studded with rings, all of which were thick bands of solid gold.

The man Malloy was screaming at had been at the fights earlier in the evening. He'd also been at Sal's when the two masked men came in with guns drawn. And he'd been there as well when those two brought another back to go in and clean out that saloon for good. His name was Al Jorgenson. Even though he towered over his boss by a good foot when they were both standing, Jorgenson gave away at least a hundred pounds to the shorter man. His scraggly blonde hair hung in greasy strips and his body trembled whenever Malloy raised his voice. All in all, he looked like a scarecrow trembling in the fat man's wind.

"I . . . I saw them go into the saloon and then they came back . . ." Jorgenson repeated.

"I heard that part!"

"After they came back here and spoke to you, they went to Sal's just like you told them and they took one of the Cummings brothers with them. When they went back into Sal's, they surrounded the place and went in. None of them are coming back."

Malloy hopped onto the edge of his large oak desk and snatched a cigar from a box. After chewing off the end and spitting it at Jorgenson's feet, he fired up a match and got the cigar burning. After drawing in a breath of the foul smoke, he let it out and snarled, "You saw all this . . . and you didn't do anything about it?"

"Y-you tol' me to watch and report to you. That's all I did."

"Yeah, well that's awful brave of you." Malloy dropped off the desk and started pacing his office. "I told those two, specifically told them, to try and get the money that they were offered. Didn't you hear me when I told them that?"

"Yes, I—"

"And after that . . . after getting my order to wait . . . they went back in there anyway." Thinking back to the last time he'd seen the gunmen alive, Malloy knew that his order to give in to the man at the saloon had stung the shotgunners' pride. Being familiar with violent men, Malloy knew that his hired guns felt beaten after being driven away with nothing but words like that. Then, there was also the other matter.

"That one you told me about," Malloy said. "The one who made the offer. He said he was Clint Adams?"

"Something like that."

"Do you think that's true, or was that just bullshit?"

Jorgenson furrowed his brow and put his fingers to his chin as if he was trying to mimic someone thinking rather than actually going through the process himself. After rolling his eyes into his head and pondering dramatically for a little while, he eventually came up with his conclusions. "I don't know. Maybe."

Malloy chewed on the end of his cigar and let some more of the smoke filter through his sinuses and then back out of his nostrils. He then turned on the scrawnier man and gave Jorgenson a vicious backhand that rivaled many of the blows that had been delivered at that evening's fights.

"Just when I think you can't be any more worthless, you go and say something like that," Malloy raged. "It wasn't a very hard question. Do you think that man is lying or is he really the Gunsmith?"

Jorgenson's hand went to his face. For a moment, he seemed to be fighting back tears before finally rising up to his full height and staring straight ahead. "I didn't see what happened inside, but I got a look at how he killed Chester in the alley behind the place. He was fast, Mister Malloy. He was real fast."

"Chester was a back-shooting son of a bitch. Someone was bound to kill him sooner or later."

"But he had the drop on that man. Had the shotgun right to his head, and still that other one turned things around and killed Chester dead."

This seemed to satisfy Malloy for the moment. Rather than take another shot at Jorgenson, he concentrated on his cigar and paced around his office. The room was small, but lavishly furnished with a fine, dark red rug and paintings on the wall. A crystal lamp sat on the edge of his desk and another lantern hung on the wall next to a portrait of a nude woman reclining on a bed of roses.

After flicking a thick bunch of ashes into a glass ashtray, Malloy turned and stared out of the room's only window. "You know why I'm so mad about all of this?" he asked.

Not one to know when to shut up, Jorgenson answered, "Probably because you wanted to—"

"It's because I wanted to give this man some time to pay us the money he offered. That gun I hired . . . the one who brought in the others . . . what was his name?"

"Corbett, sir."

"Right, right. That Corbett was too proud to take money instead of blood. But what he don't know is that we're in business to make money. All the blood we spill is for the same reason. You think I fix those fights for my health?"

"No, sir."

"Hell no. I do it for money. And when people gamble, they don't mind parting with their money. Most folks even expect to lose. And if people would listen to me and follow my lead, then we'd all be making money. It's men like Corbett and that goddamned fighter who get wrapped up in pride and fail to see the big picture. You understand, Jorgenson?"

"Y-yes, sir."

"Of course you don't. That's why you follow orders. People get too proud and don't follow orders, they wind up getting killed. Just like that fool Corbett."

Clenching the smoldering cigar between his teeth, Malloy rocked back and forth on his heels with his hands clasped behind his back. The glass reflected his own face laid over the view of what lay beyond it. Malloy's small dark eyes darted back and forth between both images, unsure as to where they should settle.

"Yes, indeed," Malloy continued. "Pride'll kill any man. Even a famous one."

TEN

Rayburn's home was little more than a collection of half-rotted boards held together by rusty nails. Every breeze that passed rattled the structure with icy fingers that slid through the entire house. When Rayburn began fixing a fire in an old pot-bellied stove, Clint's first impulse was to stop him to keep the entire place from burning down. But when the heat began to spread into the room, the risk of fire seemed a fair price to pay.

Besides the main room, which served as kitchen, dining room, living area and the boy's bedroom, there was only one other door, which led to another bedroom roughly the size of a large outhouse. It was into that room that the blonde woman went to as soon as she entered the house.

"I wish I had more to offer you by way of thanks," Rayburn said with an apologetic shrug. "But what you see is pretty much all I got." The fire was going strong now and Rayburn set an iron teapot on top of the stove. "I am thankful, though. And if you need a place to stay for the night, you can surely stay here."

"Actually," Clint said, "I don't think it's a good idea for anyone to be staying here. Not if this Malloy knows where you live."

"He knows. He's the one that set me up with this place."

43

"How generous of him," Clint said as another stray breeze rattled every wall at once.

Rayburn eased himself down onto a chair that somehow managed to hold together under his weight. "We ain't gonna stay here for much longer, though. That's why I did what I did at the fight."

"I was just about to ask you about that. Besides knowing that you're a damn good fighter in some kind of trouble, I don't know much else."

"Well, I used to do some fighting down in San Francisco . . . must'a been close to ten years ago now. Made a pretty good name for myself fighting on docks and even in a hall or two. Even got a shot at the champ once."

Snapping his fingers, Clint felt a surge of excitement as his whole face lit up. "I knew I saw you somewhere before! You fought George Slattery, didn't you?"

Rayburn nodded, a wistful smile drifting across his face. "Sure did. Nearly killed each other, but it was one of the best fights I had in them days. You saw that one?"

"I certainly did. I remember not being able to decide if I should be proud for witnessing such a fight or ashamed for standing by and watching that kind of carnage. Hell, I thought for sure that one ended both of your careers."

"Nah. When you become a fighter, you learn to take yer lumps and move on. But I don't mind tellin' you that those were some pretty damn big lumps." Even thinking about that fight, Rayburn had to rub his eyes and forehead as though the dried blood and bruises there were actually leftovers from that bout. "Slattery kept touring the circuit and me . . . well, you see where I'm at.

"About a year and a half ago, I moved up here into the high country because Malloy was paying for fighters to come and work in towns between Colorado, Wyoming, and Utah. He paid real good and the crowds were bigger than a lot of the backroom fights I had in California."

Absorbed in the conversation, Clint pulled up another rickety chair and sat down. The wooden frame squeaked and moaned, but held him up. "What about New York? I thought all the big-time fights went there."

"That's true enough, but New York is a bit rough for anyone who wants a career that lasts more than one or two years. Unless you're the champ, you get thrown into some nasty bouts. Friends of mine that went east lost eyeballs, ears, fingers, and even their noses before they packed it in. They got better houses than me, but I'd rather have all my parts present and accounted for."

Clint shook his head as the teapot started whistling on top of the stove. Like anyone else, he'd seen a few boxing matches and heard about the occasional title defense in the newspapers, but he never really thought about what it took to be one of those fighters. Thinking back to the last few matches he'd seen, most of them were bare-knuckle bloodlettings held in the middle of a crowd in an old building somewhere or in some empty lot. The fights in San Francisco were held on a pier as were the ones in New York.

There were times when Clint had seen those fighters do everything but kill their opponents. Both men usually walked away spitting blood and teeth, but none of it seemed unusual since it was all a part of the game. Clint had enjoyed watching the brutal spectacle. He'd even enjoyed betting on them just as much as he enjoyed betting on cards or even the occasional horse race. But now, as he watched Rayburn limp from one end of the shanty hut to another on legs that wobbled beneath his muscular frame, Clint looked back on those fights with new eyes.

"Is Malloy your manager, then?" Clint asked.

Rayburn busied himself pouring some hot water into a tin mug and fixing a cup of coffee. "More of a slave driver, if you ask me. He doesn't much care what happens in his fights so long as there's a crowd watching them. I seen friends of mine come home with holes in their faces 'cause some punk snuck nails in his gloves. That's why I prefer to only go bare-knuckled. Them gloves are so thin, it doesn't make much difference anyways."

"And was I right before?"

"About me supposed to be the one lying on that floor this evenin'?" Stirring the coffee with a dirty spoon, Rayburn nodded. "Right as rain. Calhoun's a great fighter and if he'd have been fighting like he meant it, he might have beaten me fair and square."

"So what happened?"

"The simple fact is that Malloy makes a lot of money betting on his fighters, but he can make even more when he knows for certain who the winner will be."

"Not a very complex scheme."

"No, but it's worked for him for some time now and he doesn't much appreciate it when his fighters don't go along with it."

"Has anyone ever gone against him before?"

Rayburn was obviously rattled by some memory sparked from that question. "Yes, there's been one or two."

"What happened to them?"

"Let's just say that they weren't lucky enough to have the Gunsmith in their corner. I doubt anyone'll find their bodies anytime soon. Not unless there's a summer hot enough to thaw out that entire mountain range."

ELEVEN

Just then, the door at the back of the room swung open and the blonde woman stepped out from her bedroom. The boy, who'd been sitting on his bed in the corner, jumped to his feet and ran to her side.

She was wearing a clean, simple cotton dress that was the color of a summer sky. Her hair fell down over her shoulders and when she moved, her body wriggled invitingly beneath her clothing. Now that she wasn't covered from head to toe in coats, she could be seen for the curvaceous woman that she truly was. Full, round breasts bounced with each of her steps and her wide, generous hips twitched under the blue cotton. When the dim light in the room caught her skin, it accented the shape of her face, the small pointed chin as well as the tiny, upturned nose.

"My sister never did like me fighting," Rayburn said as she walked toward the stove. "Never seemed to mind the money, though."

She opened her hand and swatted Rayburn on the back of the head. "That's right," she said. "And I'm such a bad person that I've spent the last five years cooking for you and sewing up that fool head of yours every time one of those bulls stampedes over it." When she looked at Clint, her entire demeanor changed. A smile lit up her face and

47

she extended the hand she'd just used to smack her brother. "By the way, my name is Myra. If it was up to my brother, I'm sure you might have gotten a proper introduction in a week or so."

Clint stood and took her hand. Her skin was just as soft as it looked. And somehow, despite the freezing wind and drafty house, her flesh managed to stay just as warm as her smile.

"Pleased to meet you. I'm Clint Adams."

"When you said that before, I didn't come close to believing you."

This time, it was Rayburn who seemed about ready to swat his sibling. "Myra!"

"But then I saw you move," she continued, making no effort to hide the way she looked him up and down. Myra's eyes drank in every detail of Clint's face and body as she slowly worked her way closer to him. "I saw you stand up to those gunmen and help us get out of that place with our lives."

She was close enough to him now that Clint could smell the natural sweetness of her skin and the fresh-air scent of her hair. With her hands tracing over his shoulders just hard enough to raise the hair on the back of Clint's neck, Myra leaned forward and kissed him gently on the cheek. Her lips were soft and moist, lingering just for a second before she walked back to the stove.

"Thank you, Clint," she said.

Clint's mind raced through all the times he'd seen her. At first, he'd just been savoring the memories as a way to prolong the feeling she gave him when they'd kissed. But then, something else came to mind. It was the first time he'd seen her at the fights that evening. Only, it hadn't been with Rayburn, but with one of the other fighters who'd nearly gotten his head taken off in a preliminary bout.

"How many other fighters do you help out, Myra?" Clint asked.

Setting a large pot on the stove, she reached into a sack

on the floor and pulled out a raw potato. Using a knife that had been on the table, she started cutting up the potato and letting the pieces fall into the boiling water. "What do you mean?" she replied.

"I saw you at the fights tonight with another boxer. Actually, you and the boy were there helping him out of the ring."

"That would've been Sal's son, Kyle," Rayburn said. "Myra helps him out as a favor to Sal. We get free meals and drinks that way."

Clint turned to Rayburn and asked, "So why go against Malloy now? This can't be anything too new. If you've been working with him for this long, he's probably asked you to do this before."

"Actually, I was just gonna mention that part," Rayburn said. "The reason is because, until now, I haven't had anywhere else to run to."

"And now you do, huh? When were you going to leave for this place?"

Rayburn shifted in his seat and downed the rest of his coffee. "It's a place up in the Rockies and it's just small enough to keep us out of sight no matter how hard Malloy looked for me. All I got to do is get there without him following me. It's a dangerous ride up the side of a mountain. And I was plannin' on headin' out in about an hour."

That was when Clint scanned the small room for all the pieces to the puzzle that had previously been missing. First, there was the fact that the normally anxious boy had been keeping to himself ever since they'd arrived. Now he could see that that was because the boy had been quietly gathering all of his possessions into a small valise. As far as Myra being so calm after witnessing a gunfight, Clint could now see the trunk in the next room through the open door. She was packed and ready to go, only minutes away from putting Brookins and all its dangers behind her.

And for Rayburn himself, the big fighter looked dead

serious when he'd said those last words to Clint. Compared to starting a ride up into the mountains in this kind of bitter cold and pitch black, getting shot at by a few quick-tempered gunmen wasn't hardly as dangerous.

"Are you crazy?" Clint asked once he decided that Rayburn wasn't joking about the whole thing. "It's bad enough to try and ride up some of those trails, but in the middle of the night?"

Rayburn nodded gravely. "I know, but night's the only edge we can get to cover our trip . . . at least the beginning of it. If Malloy's men track us right from here, then we might as well not even bother going. At least with a head start, we can get a big enough lead to cover our trail, maybe set some false ones. You bought us a whole week . . ."

Shaking his head, Clint stood up and said, "Malloy couldn't even wait a few minutes before sending out some more of his men, so there's no reason to think he's considering my offer. Hell, I'm surprised nobody else has come out here yet. I know men like him. You showed him up in public and after something like that, he'll be out to put you down. That's not the type of thing you shake off with a few false trails. My guess is that he probably already knows where you'll be heading anyway."

"Then . . . I don't suppose," Rayburn said haltingly, "that you'd be willing to come with us?"

Clint started to say something else to the fighter right at that moment. He wanted to thank the boxer for the hospitality, say his good-byes, and be on his way. But then he saw that every eye in the place was turned his way. Rayburn, Myra, and even the boy were waiting for him to speak, with hope in their eyes strong enough for Clint to feel it pouring over him.

"Aw, hell," Clint said under his breath. "Maybe we're all crazy."

TWELVE

If he was going to go along with this plan to trek up into the mountains, Clint knew that he needed to move Rayburn and his family as soon as possible. Although a remote cabin at the end of some hidden path amid the heights of the Rockies wouldn't have been his first choice, it was a hell of a lot better than Rayburn's home, which was surely about to be attacked by Malloy's men.

As much as he wanted to get moving, Clint knew that the journey ahead was dangerous enough and would be even more so without resting up first. So after he and Rayburn got Myra and the boy ready to go, Clint checked them into his hotel where he could at least keep tabs on them while they all prepared for their excursion into the mountains.

The owner of the hotel knew just as well as anybody else in Brookins just how power hungry Malloy was. He'd also heard about the shoot-out at Sal's and agreed to keep Rayburn's presence at the hotel a secret. According to the register, the new occupants of room number eight were Mr. and Mrs. Gleeson from Kansas.

After everyone was situated in their rooms, Clint made his way back to his and shut the door behind him. For a few moments, he just stood there with his eyes closed, swearing he could still hear echoes of all the commotion that had filled his head for the last several hours.

The roar of the crowd at the fights was a dull rush in his mind. Raised voices screamed through his memories. And above it all, there was the sound of doors crashing open, gunshots, explosions . . .

When he opened his eyes again, Clint found himself sitting on the edge of his bed with his hands pressed against his forehead. He took a deep breath, held it for a second, and then let it out. It was a simple thing, but one that was easy to forget when so many crises heaped themselves onto his shoulders at once. Being used to dealing with life-and-death matters as a way of life, Clint found that just stopping and taking a nice, quiet breath could sometimes make all the difference in the world.

And, just like all the other peaceful moments he'd been able to get lately, this one lasted for about a minute and a half.

The sound started out as one of the echoes rattling through his tired ears. But then it took on a different kind of rhythm: slow, yet insistent. When he concentrated a little bit, he could tell that the sound was not a memory, but something happening at that moment. He waited in the silence for it to come back again. Just when he was about to forget about it and go to sleep, it came back as a gentle rapping on his door.

Now that he'd heard it and knew what it was, Clint wanted nothing more than for it to go away. Afraid to make another sound that would let whoever it was know he was inside, Clint sat perfectly still. But the knocking came back again, this time just a little bit louder.

Grudgingly, Clint got to his feet and checked to make sure his gun was at his side. Only then did he pull back the latch and open the door a crack.

The hallway was empty, which immediately set Clint's instincts on full alert. His grip tightened around the handle of his gun as he quickly looked from side to side. Only when his eyes caught movement just beneath his field of vision did Clint's muscles relax.

Sitting with his back against the wall right next to Clint's door, was Rayburn's young nephew. The boy sat with his knees drawn up tightly against his chest and his face held low to form a defensive ball. One hand was wrapped around his knees and the other was frozen in mid-air before it had gotten a chance to knock one more time.

Clint checked the hall one last time and found no trace of anyone. The boy was looking up at him with wide, frightened eyes, his mouth hanging slightly open.

"What can I do for you?" Clint asked.

The boy looked too scared to talk. Clint hunkered down next to him and shifted so that his pistol was hidden behind the door frame. "I never caught your name. Mine's Clint."

"I know who you are," the boy squeaked. "I heard Uncle Ed talking about you. He said you killed men." Just then, the boy's complexion turned white and he looked as though he was expecting a whipping. "I . . . I mean you kill bad men. He told me you could help us."

"I'm not a killer by trade, but I guess your uncle isn't too far off the mark. Sometimes a man has to do bad things if he doesn't have any other choice."

The boy seemed to ponder that for a few seconds before he pushed himself up against the wall and got to his feet. Holding his hand out in front of him, he straightened his back and held his chin up high. "My name's Danny. I'm nine years old."

Clint took the boy's hand and shook it firmly. "Good to meet you, Danny. Shouldn't you be in bed right about now?"

"I wanted to ask you somethin'."

"Go ahead."

"Are you gonna take us into the mountains like Uncle Ed says?"

The sound of it still seemed crazy to Clint. After all, he'd come into town hoping for nothing more than to relax for a few days and already he'd killed three men and was about to trek up into the Rocky Mountains. "Yeah," he said grudgingly. "We'll all be heading up there in the morning. That's why you need to get some rest."

Danny turned as though he was about to walk back to his room when he stopped and looked back over his shoulder at Clint. He started to say something, waited, and then turned back around again.

"What else is bothering you, Dan?" Clint asked.

Like a twirling piece on top of a music box, the kid turned around again and stared down at the floor. "You're gonna go see those men again, aren't you?"

"Why do you think that?"

" 'Cause I heard you talking to them. Back at that saloon, after I was supposed to leave, I heard you tell them that you'd pay them. That means you'll go to see them again, doesn't it?"

"Yes, Danny," Clint said. "I'll probably be seeing those men again before too long."

"Can you do something for me, Mister Adams?"

"I can sure try."

"Kill the men that hurt Kyle. Ma says those men hurt Kyle so much that he won't never be the same again."

Before Clint could ask the boy what he was talking about, Danny turned and ran down the hall. The door to his room came open and after he stepped inside, Myra walked out and shut the door.

"Sorry about that, Mister Adams," she said once she'd walked up to him. "Sometimes Danny talks too much." Looking between him and his room, she asked, "Can I please come inside? I need to talk to you."

"Talk about what?"

"This," she said as she wrapped her arms around his neck and kissed him so deeply on the lips that she all but stole Clint's breath from him.

THIRTEEN

Clint's first impulse was to ask Myra what she was doing and, more importantly, why she was doing it at this particular moment. But after that impulse faded, his next one was to wrap his arms around the beautiful woman and return the affection she was showering upon him.

Her lips were soft and hot against his and her tongue probed urgently into his mouth. Once they'd backed into Clint's room, she reached behind and slammed his door shut. Myra stepped back and reached down to unfasten her dress and let it drop to the floor in a pile around her feet. She stood there in front of him, wearing nothing but a lace bodice and boots that laced all the way up to her knees.

Clint stepped forward and slid his hands around her waist, but managed to keep himself from kissing her again. "What's this about, Myra?" he asked.

"I would think you'd know damn well what this is about. You're a strong, handsome man," she said while moving her hands over his chest and unbuttoning his shirt. "And I'm a woman. As for the rest . . ." Moving even closer, she pressed her hips against his, grinding against his hardness and nibbling his earlobe. "Just let your instincts take over."

Her hair smelled like a fresh breeze and the scent of

her body mingled with lilac water to create an aroma that tugged at the primal center of Clint's being. His hands went automatically for her bodice, pulled it apart and threw it to the floor. Then he let his fingers roam over her body, tracing up and down the smooth contours of her flesh and brushing gently along the sides of her breasts.

"Mmmm," she purred. "I've been thinking of feeling your hands on me since I saw you at the saloon. The way you took on those killers . . ." Wriggling in his grasp, she leaned her head back and smiled up at him with her eyes closed. "I've never seen anything so exciting in all my life."

Just then, her touch became more urgent as she worked the buckle on Clint's belt. Myra's breath started to speed up and when she let it out, it came from her in hot, panting gasps. After all but tearing the jeans from Clint's body, she lowered herself to her knees and reached out to grasp his rigid penis in both hands. She stroked him gently at first, but then began to speed up as her need for him grew even more urgent.

Myra knew just where to touch him and exactly how to do it so that Clint forgot about all the questions he'd wanted to ask. There was nothing else in his mind anymore besides the need to feel her body. All he could think about was his body's craving for her flesh upon his own. And just when her hand broke contact with his skin, she wrapped her lips around the head of his cock and sucked him loudly, devouring every inch of him until her lips were tightly wrapped around the base of his shaft.

Savoring the feel of her moist lips sliding up and down the length of his cock, Clint reached down to run his fingers through Myra's golden hair, enjoying the feel of her head bobbing back and forth. The wet sounds her mouth made seemed to fill the room, soon to be joined by his moaning.

She slid him out of her mouth and then began to lick his penis as though it was a stick of candy. When she looked up at him, a wide, naughty smile illuminated Myra's face.

"Did you like that?" she asked in a soft, husky voice.

Clint put his hands on her arms and guided her up to her feet. He then moved around behind her and slid his arms around her waist. Moving his mouth up to her ear, Clint nudged aside her blonde locks and ran his tongue along her neck, tracing a line up over her ear. He then blew on her skin, which sent a chill all the way down her spine.

"I liked it very much," he said softly. He could feel his rigid pole pressing against Myra's soft, plump buttocks. Pressing himself against her a little harder, he asked, "Do you like that?"

She reached up to run her fingers through Clint's hair as her body seemed to melt into his. Leaning her head back, Myra let her hair fall against Clint's shoulder while squirming in just the right way to get Clint even harder.

In a flash, she'd turned herself around and was looping her arms up over Clint's head. After locking her fingers behind his neck, she held him tightly and kissed him passionately on the mouth.

Clint stepped out of his clothes, which had formed a pile around his ankles, and moved Myra closer to the bed. The black leather of her boots made the skin of her legs look all the more smooth and creamy. She moaned slightly as he cupped her bottom and lifted her up off her feet so he could set her down on top of the mattress.

She was unwilling to let him go, even as she began to pull him down on top of her. Myra's hair spilled down onto the mattress in a golden cascade and when she was fully on her back, it lay beneath her head like a shimmering pillow. Finally, she unlocked her fingers and let Clint rise above her. When she took a breath, her breasts rose up, nipples hardening as they got nearer to his skin.

Clint looked down at her body, all spread out beneath him like an erotic offering. Her nipples were large and the same shade of pink as the lips between her legs. The thatch of hair covering those lips was the same shade of gold as the hair on her head. She squirmed languidly beneath him as though she could feel his eyes upon her like two fingers tickling her skin.

"I can't wait any longer," she said. "Make love to me."

Clint lay down beside her and moved his hands along Myra's flesh. She shifted onto her side as well, hooking one leg over Clint's body and positioning herself so that he merely had to push his hips forward to penetrate her. When he did, Clint let out a satisfied groan as her damp warmth enclosed him. He reached around to grab her bottom with one hand and when he did, she dug her nails into his back and began grinding against him in search of her own pleasure.

Once they found their rhythm, their bodies moved together in a serpentine dance that twisted their limbs around each other until it seemed as though every part of him was touching every part of her, sending every nerve in their bodies on fire.

Clint nearly rolled off the bed altogether when she positioned herself on top of him and straddled his hips with her legs on either side. Propping herself up with her hands flat against his chest, Myra bounced up and down on top of his pole, leaning her head back and moaning softly so that only Clint could hear her crying out in ecstasy.

As she rode him, Clint ran his hands over Myra's breasts, feeling them bounce and sway with the motion of her body. He then felt her sides as she writhed on top of him and her stomach as she breathed in and out with quick, shallow breaths. Finally, his hands came to rest upon her hips and then around to cup her buttocks as she moved back and forth, rubbing her most sensitive spots against his hard cock.

Suddenly, Myra's quiet moaning came to a stop and her back stiffened. Her legs clamped in tightly, squeezing him in between them as she tightly closed her eyes and started thrusting her hips back and forth with long, forceful strokes. Every time she took him all the way inside of her, Myra bit into her lower lip as though that was the only thing keeping her from screaming out at the top of her lungs.

Clint could feel his own pleasure building up and as her pace got quicker, he found it more and more difficult to keep from screaming himself. Although he didn't really have a reason to stay so quiet, it was that one bit of restraint that made all the other sensations that much more intense. The more he wanted to make a sound, the harder it was to hold back. The more he held back, the sensations of her hands on his chest, her legs around his hips, her weight on top of him, the warm dampness of his body penetrating hers all got stronger until finally he couldn't hold back any longer.

This time, it was Clint who nearly bit into his bottom lip. Instead, he ground his teeth together as wave after wave pleasure washed over his entire body. Myra was leaning back now as her own orgasm swept through her system. She reached back to support herself by placing her hands on Clint's thighs and arching her back until her hair tickled his knees.

The sight of her body displayed for him like that was there the instant Clint opened his eyes. She was breathtaking in that position, but Clint was too exhausted to do much more than admire the view. Judging by the way she fell forward and rolled off to the side once her climax had subsided, Myra felt just as tired as he was.

Too fatigued to even slip beneath the covers, they managed to get into each others arms before losing consciousness altogether. For those few restful hours, Clint thought of nothing but the beating of his heart and Myra's steady breaths.

FOURTEEN

Clint was up and out of bed minutes before the sun crested the horizon. Although his body only wanted to crawl under the covers and collapse for another few hours, his mind knew that if he was going to get Rayburn and his family out of town safely, it would have to be done soon. Every minute he wasted allowed Malloy and his killers to get that much closer.

Stumbling out of his room and making his way down the stairs, Clint was greeted by the scents of fresh coffee and frying bacon. He entered the dining room to find Rayburn, Myra, and Danny all sitting at a table already digging into their breakfasts.

"Hope you saved me some of that," Clint said as he dropped into a chair next to Myra.

Rayburn seemed to be the most alert of all of them and he reached across the table to slug Clint good-naturedly on the shoulder. "Sure did, friend," he said, nearly sending Clint over onto his back with the impact of his fist. "They wanted to get you up earlier, but I told 'em to let you sleep. You had a big day yesterday, after all."

"Seems to me you had a hard time of things, yourself," Clint pointed out. "Or did I just dream that match you had last night?"

Rayburn waved his hand dismissively. "Oh, that was

just another day at work for me. I get my head beat in for a living. Besides, knocking that boy on his ass was almost worth all the trouble just to see the look on Malloy's face when Calhoun's back hit the floor."

Sitting next to his uncle with his head held low and his back hunched over, Danny looked as though he had the weight of the world riding on his narrow young shoulders. "Can I be excused?" he asked.

Myra watched the boy with concern. She started to lean in closer to him, but before she could say anything to her son, Rayburn's voice boomed across the table.

"If yer done eatin', why don't you start bringing our bags downstairs? Be quick about it and I'll let you ride up front in the wagon."

The boy moved with all the excitement of a slug inching its way across a patch of dry mud. His feet shuffled over the floorboards and could soon be heard clomping up the stairs. Clint waited until Danny was out of earshot before signaling the waitress for a cup of coffee and looking over to Myra.

"Danny paid me a little visit last night," Clint said. "Just before you came and got him, he knocked on my door and asked me a question."

"I'm sorry about that," Myra said. "I hope he didn't disturb you or anything."

"No, not at all. Actually, I got a little distracted and nearly forgot about it until right this instant." Clint gave her a little wink and noticed how quickly Myra dropped her eyes away from him.

Just then, the waitress came over with a plate of food and set it in front of Clint. The platter consisted of a ham steak, a generous helping of eggs, thick cuts of toast, and fried potatoes. The coffee was a definite step up from the swill he'd been drinking in the last few towns and all of those tastes combined were almost enough to make him forget about all the other troubles that were brewing.

After waiting long enough for Clint to dig into his meal, Rayburn said, "I think I know what you're talking about.

He said something to me about wanting to see you. Something about Kyle."

"That's right," Clint said between bites. "The bartender's son. What happened to him?"

Rayburn snorted as though mentioning the other man's name deserved an immediate retaliation. "Kyle ain't nothin' but a used-up bum. And the fact that he's five years younger than me tells you just how much of a bum he is to have used himself up so damn quickly."

Myra reached out to swat Rayburn on the arm. "That'll be enough of that! It's not polite to talk like that."

"I forgot . . . it ain't right to speak ill of the dead."

That comment earned Rayburn yet another taste of the back of his sister's hand, which he weathered with a good-humored smile. "You'll have to forgive my sis," he said. "Somehow, she's got a soft spot in her heart for this dried-up pug who thinks it's part of a boxer's career to get himself killed every other week. You mentioned last night that you saw his fight."

Clint searched for a polite way to phrase his comments on it since Myra was there, but he couldn't think of much else to say besides, "It wasn't pretty."

Rayburn laughed hard enough for his stomach to rattle the table. If not for the smile on his face, someone might have mistaken the sound for a grizzly bear coughing up a hairball. "Ain't that the truth? It surely wasn't pretty at all, now was it?"

After the laughter died down, Clint said, "Why is Danny concerned about him? He mentioned something about Kyle getting hurt by some men. Do you know what he's talking about?"

Myra looked up somberly, forcing the smile off of her brother's face with nothing more than a sideways glance mixed in with just the right amount of anger in her eyes. Slowly, she turned toward Clint and met his gaze. "Kyle went against Malloy as soon as he heard my brother mention that he was planning on doing the same."

FIFTEEN

"Poor bastard," Rayburn interrupted. "If Kyle wasn't so stupid, I'd almost feel sorry for him." The boxer ordered another pot of coffee to be brought to the table and then continued with what he was saying. "I was talking to a bunch of the boys . . . you know, other fighters and such . . . and Kyle happened to be there as well. I was letting off steam about how we do all the fighting and Malloy gets rich off of all the blood and teeth that we leave on all them dirty floors.

"That's when I said I was gonna scrape up some money to bet on myself in a fight when Malloy was all set to win. That way, the odds against me would be bigger and I could walk away with enough to get out of this game for good. Seems he was pretty sick of Malloy too, only he didn't wait until I was set to go on my own plan. Hell, he didn't even bother telling anyone what he was gonna do. He just goes on to take some kid down that was supposed to win in a penny-ante fight held in a back room, which didn't accomplish much else besides get Malloy mad enough to kill."

"So Malloy sends out his men to bring Kyle around the hard way," Clint said.

Rayburn nodded. "Hard way is right. It would'a been kinder to just put a bullet in the guy's head, but that ain't exactly Malloy's style to do anything the kind way. Instead, he broke Kyle down so far that he'll never be the same again. Boy's got no more pride. Licks Malloy's boots without even wanting to do it. He shouldn't be fighting no more."

"Then what do you have against him?" Clint asked. "Sounds to me like you're glad he got hurt. Don't fighters stick together, or is it pretty much time to fend for yourself?"

The boxer's eyes narrowed and all the humor drained from his face. For a second, the silence at the table was uncomfortable and bordering on hostile. When Rayburn leaned forward, it appeared as if he might actually take a swing at Clint. Instead, he locked eyes with the other man and lowered his voice to a menacing snarl.

"I see where you're going with this, Mister Adams, and I don't much appreciate it. I'll help anyone else as much as I can, but when Kyle went off half-cocked like that he made Malloy look real hard at *every* fighter he hired. When Malloy started digging, he probably found out there was something else going on that he didn't know about; someone who put ideas into Kyle's little brain.

"And when Malloy realized that, he started cracking down on all of us. He watched us like a hawk and he still does . . . all because some stupid kid couldn't keep himself in line."

Myra put her arm on her brother's and patted him consolingly. "Eddie, it's not that bad . . ."

"Yes it *is* that bad," Rayburn snapped. "We weren't supposed to leave until winter was over and even now, we've got killers breathing down our necks. Hell, we probably shouldn't have put off running this long!"

More than ever, Clint wanted to get Rayburn and his family on their way and out of Malloy's reach. Once that was done, there were other matters that required his attention. "You do need to get out of town for a while . . . maybe longer," Clint said. "But what happens after that? I mean, you can't stay in the mountains forever."

Settling back into his chair, Rayburn shot a glance over his shoulder as the door to the hotel opened and then slammed shut. Clint tensed for a moment as well, but it was only another one of the guests coming in through the lobby.

"I've got enough supplies to last a good while," Rayburn said. "After that, we can come down out of the mountains using a different trail that'll lead us to any of three other towns. Using a high road like that gives us a lot more options on where we end up. From there . . ." Shrugging, the big man tried not to look at his sister and tried even harder not to think about his nephew. ". . . from there, we'll just have to wait and see. Maybe we'll head west."

"Just keep running, huh?" Clint asked.

"Yeah, unless you've got a better idea. Unless you haven't noticed, I'm not much of a gunfighter and I'm too damn poor to hire good protection."

"I'll try not to take too much offense from that last comment, Rayburn," Clint said with a wry grin.

Finally, the serious mask the fighter had been wearing cracked to show the man that had been there before. "Oh, uh . . . sorry about that. I just meant—"

"I know what you meant," Clint said, letting the bigger man off the hook. After shoveling in the rest of his breakfast as fast as he could without choking on it, Clint swigged the rest of his coffee and threw some money on the table. "One thing you were definitely right about is the fact that we need to get you out of here as soon as possible. I'm pretty sure I bought you folks enough time to get out of here and on your way into the Rockies before Malloy has a chance to follow you, but it's best if we don't take any risks."

Just then, the front door to the hotel opened and slammed shut again. This time, it was Danny who came running inside as though his britches were on fire. "I'm . . . I'm all through bringing the bags down," the boy said breathlessly. "At least . . . all the ones I could carry."

Rayburn pushed away from the table and stood up.
"Good job. Now let's get the hell out of here while we
still got the whole day ahead of us." Once they were outside by the wagon, Rayburn asked, "You following on
yer own horse, Adams, or are you riding shotgun with
Danny?"

Clint noticed the way that question seemed to spark an
excited glint in the boxer's eyes that made him resemble
a giant-sized version of his nephew. Grinning, Clint said,
"If I didn't know any better, I'd say that you're anxious
to meet up with Malloy again."

"Hell yeah, I'm anxious," Rayburn said while getting
to his feet. "Especially since I'm prepared this time." With
a proud flourish, Rayburn moved his hulking arm inside
the wagon to pull out a shotgun that had been all but
hidden beneath a stack of blankets.

SIXTEEN

Clint moved around where Danny was standing and headed straight for Rayburn. The kid was standing next to a battered old wagon that had been pulled up next to a pile of luggage on the boardwalk. Before they got too close to the kid, Clint turned and put his back to him. "Listen up, Rayburn, and listen good," he said. "I understand wanting to protect your own and I've listened to all that you've been through. But you'd best keep that gun of yours locked down or under the seat of that wagon."

"B . . . but I was only tryin' to—"

"I know what you were trying to do and I appreciate your help. It would be more help, though, if you just keep watch on your family and make sure you handle that wagon as we start riding up that mountain. Just let me worry about what to do when the shooting starts and make sure you follow my lead. You'll be no good to anyone dead, understand?"

Rayburn's first reaction was a flash of anger that drifted across his face like a passing cloud. That changed, however, as he nodded slowly and slid the gun beneath the driver's seat. "Yer right, Adams. This whole thing's just got me feelin' like a daddy bear or somethin' trying to fend off the wolves."

"That's exactly what you are," Clint said. "But even

though we made it through last night well enough, I doubt we've seen the last of Malloy's killers. And since we're surely outnumbered, we need to play to our strengths. Believe me, if we get in a scrape where I need some help knocking someone into next week, you'll be the one that'll comes through for us all."

Rayburn swelled up like a peacock and slapped Clint on the shoulder. Since he was actually trying to prove his strength this time, the friendly blow staggered Clint a few steps sideways. "Yer all right, Adams," the fighter bellowed. "And just so you know, I'm already in debt to you more than I can say."

"Don't worry," Clint said as he helped load up the wagon next to Rayburn and the boy. "I know."

SEVENTEEN

Once the wagon was ready to roll, Rayburn got it going on out of town and headed for a trail which led directly to the foot of the Rockies and up the side. Clint watched them go before hurrying down the street to the livery where he picked up Eclipse. He loaded up his things and rode off at a full gallop to catch up with Rayburn before they got too far ahead of him.

The trip out of town was actually one of the most relaxing parts of his visit to Brookins thus far. It was still early morning and the sunlight hit the mountains in just such a way as to make the snow on their sides sparkle. The pines clinging to the mountain had frozen the night before and were covered with thin sheets of ice that shimmered and glistened in the light, making the entire range of trees look as though they'd been formed out of delicate crystal.

In the open land, the sounds of the horses' hooves and wagon wheels were swallowed up almost immediately. The town was less than a mile behind them and already Clint felt like he was trekking through the desolate wilderness. Everyone else seemed absorbed in their own thoughts, making the travel that much more peaceful for Clint's racing mind.

Every so often, Clint would glance over his shoulder

to make sure that they were truly the only ones on this trail for the time being. He was fairly confident that they'd managed to get on their way before being followed, but it all still seemed to go along a bit too easily for his comfort.

The wagon had been packed with dry goods and supplies to last the family for at least a couple of weeks, possibly even as long as a month if they kept their meals small and took as much as they could from the land itself. According to Rayburn, the cabin they were headed to was remote, but still inside the tree line, which meant there would still be wood for fires and game for hunting. The ride there would take at least a couple of days.

Longer if there were any problems.

Clint was hopeful, but he wasn't about to kid himself into thinking that the trip would go off without a hitch. There would be problems, all right. Hopefully, they just wouldn't be too big to overcome.

Once they were five miles outside of town, Clint brought Eclipse up alongside the wagon. Rayburn sat in front with his massive frame slouched over and wrapped inside an old long coat. He gripped the reins loosely in his pawlike hands, only occasionally giving them a slight flick. Next to him, Danny sat bundled up in several layers of jackets and sweaters, his eyelids growing heavy from lack of sleep combined with all the fresh air. Myra was in back beneath the wagon's tarp, crowded in between several trunks and cases.

Clint got Rayburn's attention without waking up the boy. "How much trail do you suppose you've got before you start heading up the side?" he asked.

Rayburn studied the road for a few seconds and then rubbed his hands together. His forehead wrinkled as though the effort of pondering the question was enough to twist him up from the inside out. "Well, we're not headed for the closest one, but the one next to it. If we take it nice and easy, and stick to the low ground as much as possible, we should reach the base by a little after sundown. We could start climbing tomorrow mornin' or if you wanted, we could get up into the tree line for cover and start heading south from there."

"No, try to get in as much easy riding as you can. I need to head back into town and settle some business. If you let me know where you'll be making camp, I can meet you there tonight and then we can all head for the high road tomorrow."

Rayburn regarded Clint with a troubled look in his eyes. He stared down from the driver's seat as though he wanted to say something, but was afraid to do so in front of Danny and Myra. "Why don't I unhitch one of the nags and I can follow you back into Brookins? That way, whatever business you've got won't have to be handled alone."

Clint's first reaction was to put the fighter's worries to rest and assure him that he was just going back to town for something trivial. It was obvious, however, that Rayburn knew better and Clint wasn't about to insult the big man by talking down to him. "Thanks, but this is one of those things that I need to do on my own. Besides, this may be a flat stretch of trail, but it's still not something that should be driven by a woman and child."

"We could stop here while I follow you in," Rayburn said as a last-ditch offer. "You know . . . just for backup."

The truth of the matter was that Clint was sorely tempted to accept Rayburn's help. Seeing as how he had no idea what Malloy had waiting or how many men would be looking for them, the thought of going in alone was not overly attractive. But rather than let on he was thinking like that, Clint shrugged and said, "I appreciate it Rayburn, but this shouldn't take too long. You're needed here. If you don't hear from me tonight, head out tomorrow and keep an eye out. I'll catch up to you."

Rayburn gritted his teeth and nodded. "They'll be after you the minute you show your face in town."

"I know."

"And after what happened last night, they'll be ready for you. More'n likely, they'll gang up on you even worse than before. Might even ambush you outside of town coming or going."

"I know that too."

Sighing, Rayburn seemed to be pushing something down deeper inside of him. The thick muscles in his neck tensed with what was obviously a tremendous effort. "Last time I checked, Malloy had about ten or so men working for him, not to mention the fighters. This trail heads west and then hooks to the south at a fork about twenty miles ahead. We'll be camping down the south fork at a spot that's hidden behind a bunch of rocks topped off with a few stray pines. It's called Crown Pass. You'll see why when you get there."

"Thanks, Rayburn. You're a good man."

"A good man wouldn't let you head back into town alone."

"No, a good man does what he's got to do no matter what." Turning Eclipse around to head in the direction from which they'd come, Clint raised the collar on his jacket to keep the swirling, snow-laden winds from raking too far down his throat and chest. "I'll see you soon enough."

"Damn right," Rayburn said with a wave. " 'Cause if you take too long, I'll have to come tear that town apart lookin' for you and that would just throw my schedule all to hell."

Clint laughed and returned the fighter's wave. As he flicked Eclipse's reins, he looked over to see Myra staring at him from the back of the wagon. Her eyes were wide and full of fear.

A vicious wind kicked up a cloud of loosely packed snow that enveloped the wagon like a giant, ghostly fist. When she could see again, Myra was back inside the wagon, watching Clint go as though she was certain she would never set eyes on him again. For a moment, it seemed as though she would jump down off the wagon and chase after him, if only to give him a kiss before parting ways. But then Danny yelled for her from the front of the wagon, reminding her of exactly why she needed to stay.

Clint brought Eclipse to a halt and then turned around to look at her one more time. Even wrapped head to toe in dresses, coats, and other layers of clothing, she was still just as attractive to him as when she'd been lying naked in his arms. He waved to her and then tipped his hat. Even though he couldn't hear her, Clint knew she was saying something quietly to herself, directed toward his ears through the widening distance between them.

A little wisp of steam curled up from between her full, red lips and danced around her smooth face and the wisps of golden hair that had managed to peek out from under her wool hat. She then turned her attention toward her son as the wagon rumbled over the frozen soil.

Clint thought about what she might have been saying just then. It occupied his mind all the way back into Brookins, giving him something better to focus on besides what would be waiting for him there.

EIGHTEEN

The entire town of Brookins was bathed in a bright, almost heavenly light reflecting off the layers of snow and ice, giving the streets an otherworldly appearance. In any place, dawn could be a spectacular sight to behold. But when combined with newly arrived snow, frost, and ice, the purples and oranges of the sky splashed down upon the white in a breathtaking display. Eventually, the reds and oranges would shift into yellow. From there, the skies would turn bright blue, making the landscape seem clean and pure.

Dawn was a good time for poets and songwriters. Even for men with darkness in their hearts, dawn was a time to feel just as clean as the land itself. Clean, that is, until sleep lost its hold upon them and their attentions turned away from the sky and back to the plans they'd set into motion.

Randal Malloy was such a man. Although there was nobody with enough guts to tell him so to his face, he would never have argued that fact with anyone. He knew there was plenty of darkness in his heart. He could feel it swelling up from deep down inside of him like acidic bile working its way up to the back of his throat. It was hard for a man to deny something when he choked on it every day.

Malloy stood at the window of his office and watched as local townspeople began poking their heads out into the cold and shuffled about their daily lives. He'd been one of those people once, back when he'd used to scuttle through life like just another bug trying not to get beneath someone's boot. It wasn't a life that he particularly missed. And if he had to be the one wearing the boots that crushed other bugs to keep him away from that type of existence, than so be it. Malloy had no problem with crushing those who were stupid enough to get in his way.

No problem at all.

Situated on the busy corner of Second and Timber Avenues, Malloy's office got a particularly good view of the bugs as they rushed down the street and out of the saloons. With a turn of his head, he could see the sheriff's office or even the courthouse. Town Hall was only half a block away and on those rare occasions when the mood struck him, he could strain his neck to get a look at the town chapel.

Today was one of those days. Except, when Malloy looked toward the little church, he thought about the services that would be held there once he got his hands on Ed Rayburn. Actually, it would be one of Malloy's men that would get their hands dirty, but every time his employees cracked open somebody's skull, Malloy swore he could feel the blood under his fingernails.

When he caught sight of a particular someone making their way toward his office, Malloy thought he could already feel the warm wetness on his hands. The man walking slowly across the street was someone who Malloy saw as his own personal specter of death. The figure was lean and just the right height to blend seamlessly into nearly any crowd. Based on looks alone, the solitary man wasn't anything much to look at. He stood somewhere between five and a half and six feet tall. He carried himself in a simple manner with his hands tucked into the pockets of a long brown duster and his eyes all but covered beneath the narrow brim of a plain gray bowler.

He walked between the people on the street, stepping around them and avoiding contact with the subdued grace of a bit of dust that managed to always stay just out of reach. It hadn't been until just recently that Malloy was able to fully appreciate the man's quick, stealthy movements. To the impartial observer, the man just looked as though he was doing his best not to get trampled underfoot. But if anyone took the time to watch for more than a few seconds, they just might be able to tell that the figure was making his way through a group of people without once being touched by any of them and, more importantly, without ever once being noticed.

Malloy knew that man could walk down the middle of an otherwise empty street while folks sat on either side and he would be forgotten as soon as he stepped into the shadows. Not one of those people lining the street would remember much more than some plain-looking gentleman in plain-looking clothes.

And that was the beauty of the whole thing.

That man was a first-rate killer named Lawrence Krackow. He never had to think too hard about how to sneak up on his victims since, if anyone did see him coming, they wouldn't even think twice about the slender man. After he struck, Krackow wouldn't run or ride away. He would simply find a crowd of any size and get lost inside of it. After more than thirty kills, his face had yet to grace a wanted poster.

Other killers thought of Krackow as something of a legend. Half of them sat around in saloons telling secondhand stories about his more famous jobs. The other half didn't even believe he existed. None of them called him by name, however.

Among his peers, Krackow was known simply as "The Plague."

He killed like a disease: unseen, efficient and unmindful of who its victim were. Men fell to a plague just as easily as women and children. A plague didn't care who it struck down . . . and neither did Lawrence Krackow.

Krackow was the most dangerous man Malloy had ever met. Sometimes, the killer would show up out of nowhere as if he'd just appeared on the spot. The fact that Malloy had been able to spot him outside of his office at all was only because he'd summoned the killer and knew what to look for after years of practice. It was a small victory, but it brought a smile to Malloy's face all the same.

That smile disappeared when Malloy made the mistake of blinking one too many times. One instant, Krackow had been walking next to a portly old man wearing a wool vest and leather gloves. In the next, that old man was walking alone, hardly aware that anyone had been beside him at all.

When Malloy turned his head to try and pick out the killer again, there was a knock on his door, which echoed through the entire office like the dry rattle of an ax chopping down a dead tree.

Another knock.

"Should I get that?" Jorgenson asked from the next room.

"No, AL. I pay you to sit on your ass and stuff your face all day long."

Setting his fork down next to the plate of scrambled eggs he'd been working on, Jorgenson got up and hurried to the front door. Truth be told, he knew who was out there just by the sound of the knock. When he opened the door, he was careful not to meet the cold, lifeless eyes of the man waiting outside.

"Mister Malloy is waiting for you," Jorgenson said to the floor.

Krackow stepped inside and stomped the snow off his boots. When his hand came out of his pocket, he didn't let on that he'd seen Jorgenson flinch. Any other man might have chuckled at Jorgenson's twitchy display of cowardice, but not Krackow. All he did was pull the handkerchief from his coat pocket, dab it to his nose and blow.

"Could I have something hot to drink?" the killer asked.

NINETEEN

Clint's first stop as soon as he made it back into Brookins was Sal's Saloon. It was the last place he'd seen Malloy's men and it was as good a place as any to get a hot cup of coffee to thaw the ice in his veins.

On his way to the saloon, he spotted no fewer than half a dozen men who eyed him suspiciously as he rode by. He couldn't say for sure if they belonged to Malloy, but each one of those men seemed to hold his gaze for just a bit too long, their hands drifting slowly toward the guns at their hips.

As soon as Clint arrived at Sal's, he tied Eclipse outside, making sure that the rifle in the saddle holster was loaded and tucked away beneath one of the blankets of his bedroll. The water trough was nothing more than a block of ice wrapped in wood, but it didn't matter since Clint didn't plan on being inside the place for very long anyway. He pet the Darley Arabian twice on the neck and strode inside.

Since there wasn't a match being fought anytime soon, the place was fairly deserted. Rubbing his hands together, Clint took another step inside the place and looked around. It was almost as if the owners of the place didn't even expect anyone since they didn't even bother putting coals in the fire or food on the stovetop. Suddenly, Clint felt a wave of hunger hit him like a solid left hook right in the solar plexus.

"We don't really get much business when there ain't any fights on, mister," came a gruff, scratchy voice from behind the bar.

Clint spun around looking for the source of the voice, only to find an eyeful of empty chairs that were flipped upside down on top of round tables and empty seats at poker tables covered with white sheets. Actually, the more he thought about it, the worse the idea seemed to come to this place at all.

"I'm looking for Malloy," Clint said. "If he's not here, I need to know where he's at."

Clint waited for an answer. He thought about the barkeep that had been working at this place the other night and tried to decide whether or not it was that pudgy little man's voice that he'd heard a few seconds ago. The more he thought about it, the harder it was to try and nail down the voice in his mind and after a few more seconds of silence ticked by, Clint spun on his heel and started walking toward the front door.

"Where you going?" the voice asked just as Clint was about to step outside.

"I don't have time for this garbage," Clint said without turning around to look behind himself. "Either you can help me or you can't and if all you're going to do is yell at me from behind the bar, than I'll take that to mean that you can't."

This time, when the voice came back, it was a lot closer than it had been before. It gave Clint the distinct impression that whoever it was had crept up behind him. "Malloy's men are all over town today. How do I know you're not one of them?"

"First of all, if I worked for Malloy, I wouldn't exactly need to ask you where he is. And second, I wouldn't walk out of here without seeing your face if I really wanted to talk to you, which is exactly what I'm going to do. Good day."

Clint reached out to put his hand on the brass door handle. Before he could push down on the latch, he heard footsteps scurrying up from behind that weren't even trying to be sneaky. In one fluid motion, Clint turned and grabbed hold of the man rushing toward him by the throat. His other hand clamped over the handle of his gun.

The move was more reflex than anything else. And by the time Clint was able to focus on the face of the man who'd tried to rush up behind him, that person's cheeks were flushed red and his eyes were just beginning to bulge out of their sockets. His hand was wrapped around the handle of a small blade. What made the sight even more pathetic was the fact that the man's skin was already discolored with several painful-looking bruises along with a nasty cut running over his right eye.

Leaning forward slightly to get a closer look, Clint examined the features and wounds of the man in his grasp. Even though he recognized the guy, Clint still took a moment to punish him for trying to attack a man with his back turned. One more insistent squeeze was all it took to force the man to open his fist and let the boot knife clatter to the floor.

"Not exactly how you were trained, was it Kyle?" Clint sneered. "Then again, I've seen you fight. Perhaps an ambush is your best bet after all."

Twisting his hand from side to side as though he was examining a trout at the end of his fishing line, Clint looked the fighter over to check for any other weapons. As far as he could tell, Kyle wasn't wearing a gun belt. Besides the reddish tint that had just begun seeping into his skin, Kyle's face looked as though it had been kicked in by a mule. Both eyes were blackened and besides the scar over his eye, there was a cut along the side of his mouth.

"What's the matter, Kyle?" Clint asked. "Didn't you get enough of a beating the other day, or are you just a glutton for punishment?"

"T-tell Malloy that he can k-kiss my ass," Kyle stammered as he tried to sneak a few breaths from beneath Clint's grip.

"I don't work for Malloy."

"Then wh-why are you tryin' ta kill me?"

Exasperated, Clint loosened his grip and let Kyle go. While the other man was taking deep, grateful breaths, Clint sent the fallen knife under one of the nearby tables with a single well-placed kick. "In case you got your brains knocked loose, you might recall that you attacked me as soon as I stepped foot in here. That's the only reason I lifted a finger against you."

For a few seconds, Kyle was too busy collecting himself to respond. Finally, he dropped himself into a nearby chair and looked up at Clint. His face was a mixture of pain, confusion, and anger. "Malloy's always got someone new coming by here to try and whip one of us in line. How can I be sure that you're not one of 'em?"

"Because you're an idiot, that's why," came a voice from the back of the room.

Clint looked toward the source of the comment and found the portly barkeep standing in the doorway behind the bar. He was wearing a plaid flannel shirt with his sleeves rolled up and a dirty white apron tied around his waist. As he stepped forward, he clapped his hands together, which created a small cloud of dust around his midsection.

"It's a wonder you ain't gotten yerself killed already, Kyle," the barkeep mused. "That's Clint Adams. He's the one that put a bullet into those men that came after Eddie." Turning his eyes toward Clint, he asked, "What can I get for ya?"

"Something hot," Clint answered. "And put it into a canteen. I'll be leaving as soon as I find out where Mister Malloy conducts his business."

"You don't waste a lot of time, do you?"

"Well, I don't have much of it to spare. Do you know where I can find Malloy?"

This time, it was Kyle who spoke up. "I can take you there, but you might want to bring some help. Malloy's called for some outside help and when he does that, men usually turn up dead."

TWENTY

Even though Malloy had worked with the man in his office for some time and respected him greatly, he still couldn't get himself to feel comfortable around him. Krackow wasn't one of his normal employees and, as far as he knew, was nobody's friend. He was nothing but a killer, pure and simple.

"What can I get you?" Malloy asked.

Krackow blew his nose loudly into his handkerchief and pulled his coat in tighter around him. "Maybe some tea?"

Malloy was standing next to a cart in the corner of his office that was loaded down with everything from imported sherry to locally-brewed firewater. He had cut-glass decanters and polished shot glasses, but nothing even closely resembling tea. "Sorry, but I'm fresh out of that. How about some whiskey? That always does the trick for me when I need to warm up."

After taking a few moments to blow into his hands and rub them together, Krackow removed his gloves and hat. The gloves were folded neatly in half and stored in his pockets while the bowler was set down on the edge of Malloy's desk. For the first time since he'd entered the office, the killer turned his eyes toward Malloy and held them there.

Staring Krackow in the eyes was never an easy task, even for someone as practiced in intimidation as Malloy. The killer had a knack for staring straight through someone as though he was peering into his soul. It seemed as though Krackow enjoyed sending ripples of fear beneath the occasional person's skin.

After an agonizing couple of seconds, Krackow turned away. "I guess whiskey would be fine . . . if that's all you've got."

Relieved, Malloy fixed the drink and handed it over. Even without touching them, Malloy could tell that Krackow's hands were as cold as the outside of his office windows. Yet somehow, as it reached out and accepted the glass, that hand didn't shake once.

Malloy let the killer take his drink and listened as Krackow let out a slow breath.

"Good stuff, huh?" Malloy asked.

Krackow wiped his mouth with the back of his hand and stared down into the brown liquid. "What's the job?" he asked.

"Actually, I was surprised to see you so quickly. I thought you were in Wyoming settling some . . . labor problems for an associate of mine."

"I was. It took me longer to ride there than it did to kill those men." Shifting his eyes up to fix Malloy with an icy stare, he added, "And their families."

"Well, actually you couldn't have shown up at a better time. I've been having some problems of my own. A few fighters on my circuit are beginning to get a little too big for their britches and need to be taught a lesson. It started with one of the ham and eggers who went against a fix. Now there's more of them feeding ideas to the rest.

"Just the other night, one of my headliners knocked my best fighter on his ass in front of a sold-out crowd. Calhoun was supposed to be big-time material and instead he gets humiliated. I pay my fighters real well, and if they start biting the hand that feeds them, they need to realize that they'll get bitten right back."

"Sounds to me like you were backing the wrong man for the number one spot," Krackow said in a thin, rasping voice.

"That's not the point. The point is—"

"The point is that you can't have someone telling the boss what to do."

Not used to being interrupted, Malloy blinked his eyes a few times as a way to hold back his reflexive response toward such insubordination. Anybody else would have gotten a good taste of Malloy's fist for talking out of turn, but Krackow wasn't anybody else. Some folks doubted if he was even human.

"That's . . . that's right," Malloy said in a measured tone.

Krackow took another tentative sip of his whiskey and made a sour face as the alcohol burned down his throat. "I don't need to hear your whole story, sir. Just tell me who you want dead and how messy you want them to die. After that, I'll tell you my price."

"Fair enough," Malloy said, easing back into his role as businessman. As he walked around his desk, the fat man rapped on the edge of the wood with his knuckles. He paused in front of his window and stared outside, feeling suddenly ill at ease with having his back turned to the other man in his office. "Actually, the original job just got a little bigger as of the other night."

"No problem there. I'm sure you can afford the extra fee."

That was when Malloy felt a twinge in his gut. In fact, he felt it in that particular place in his gut that was connected to his pocketbook. "I called for you to take down these free-thinking fighters of mine. If they're acting up like this, I'm sure they're probably about ready to fly the coop anyway and I can't have that."

"And?"

"And what?"

"The way you're talking, even the way you're standing there tells me that there's something else you want to say.

Whatever it is, I can handle it. Just spit it out so I can get out of here and change into some warmer clothes."

Turning around and sitting behind his desk, Malloy felt a little better now that he could see the killer again. "I sent two of my men into a saloon yesterday to teach this fighter a lesson. They came back saying that the fighter had someone speaking for him and mentioned something about paying me cash to let the fighter alone for a week or so."

"Sounds like a good offer to me. If it's genuine, that is."

Again, Malloy felt his temper kick him in the stomach as a scowl crept across his face. "If the money was offered before I was made to look like a jackass in public, I might have considered it. Still, my men came back in . . . let's just say . . . less than perfect condition. I told them to wait and they went back with a third to finish off the fighter and his friend."

"I take it those three are no longer with us?" Krackow asked dryly.

"That's right."

"Now that one must have been real embarrassing for a man in your position." This time, Krackow didn't hide the sarcasm in his voice. In fact, he looked up at Malloy to watch for the reaction his comment stirred up in the other man.

To his credit, Malloy managed to keep his expression neutral. "Yes. It certainly was. The problem is this," he said while leaning forward with his hands clasped together on top of his desk. "This fighter couldn't have killed all those men. Hell, I don't think he ever owned a gun. He had a man helping him. It's this man that might pose a problem for me since I think that he's helping to smuggle my fighter out of town, which would pluck a considerable amount of money right out of my pockets."

"And we can't have that."

"No, Mister Krackow. We most definitely cannot."

The killer turned the glass around in his hand. Thus far,

he'd only taken a few little sips off the top. Placing the glass to his lips, he tilted it until the whiskey trickled over his lips and ran into his mouth. He eventually poured more down and didn't swallow until every last drop had been drained from the glass.

As soon as he drained the alcohol, Krackow balled his hand into a fist and pressed it against his lips, coughing violently until his whole upper body was convulsing with the effort. The coughing turned into a hacking rasp until finally Krackow's eyes were clenched shut. After the fit subsided, he set the glass onto Malloy's desk and cleared his throat.

"Excuse me," Krackow rasped. "But I really do prefer tea."

"The fighter from last night is named Edward Rayburn. I've heard that he's looking to leave town and he might have already done so. I want him dead. I want his family dead. I want all of their bodies found and I want everyone to know that their last moments were the worst of their lives."

Still recovering from the coughing fit, Krackow waved his hand. "Fine."

"The small-time fighter needs to go as well. He doesn't have a family, so it'll just be him I'm after."

"What about anybody with him?" Krackow asked. "I could deal with them . . . maybe deliver a few of his friends to prove your point."

"Will that cost extra?"

"Depends. If I can kill them any way I see fit . . . maybe have some fun with them, mess them up a little. I'd consider them more for myself than anything to charge you for."

Malloy had heard about some of Krackow's "fun." Two cowboys who'd stumbled into the wrong alley while Krackow was at work came up missing a year or two ago. When they were found, pieces of them were nailed to the wall of a barn. Actually, they were nailed to a barn, a saloon, and several outhouses. None of the chunks were bigger than a man's fist. Just thinking about it brought that familiar chill back to Malloy's spine. He considered paying the extra money to avoid such a gruesome sight in his town. But then again, he'd lost enough money already.

"Fine," Malloy said reluctantly. "But don't touch any more of my fighters. The rest of them are worth more to me alive."

Krackow's expression softened a bit, becoming almost wistful and serene. His eyes looked around the room as though he was already surveying the carnage he'd planned on creating. Suddenly, his eyes snapped back into focus and he turned to face Malloy once again.

"So who's this other man you talked about?" Krackow asked.

This was the part that Malloy had been waiting for. The way Krackow responded would let Malloy know whether the killer was a professional or truly crazy. "I've heard from more than one source that it's Clint Adams."

So far, Krackow's expression hadn't changed in the slightest. "Can those sources be trusted?"

Malloy nodded.

"Adams isn't a young man anymore, but if he alone took out that many of your guns, then he must still be pretty good. Killing him will cost extra, but no more than any other extra body you wanted me to throw on top of the heap." Leaning forward, the killer reached out and ran the tip of his finger along the rim of the empty whiskey glass. "If I find him and this man turns out to be Clint Adams . . . I'll kill him for free."

Yes, Malloy thought, the killer was definitely crazy.

TWENTY-ONE

Although Clint didn't much like the idea of someone else tagging along with him on his way to meet Malloy, he didn't seem to have much choice in the matter. Despite the beating he'd been given, Kyle still had some fight left in him. No matter how many times Clint had asked just for a set of directions or a point in the right direction, Kyle had insisted that he wouldn't say another word unless he could go with Clint to pay Malloy his visit in person.

Brookins was a good sized town and the more that Kyle jabbered to Clint as they walked down the street, the bigger the place actually felt. At one point, Clint felt as though he'd been walking for hours, listening to an endless stream of fight stories and rantings about Malloy and his men.

Finally, Clint turned to him and interrupted in midsentence. "Doesn't your jaw hurt after the fight?"

"A little, but I don't mind—"

"I know you don't mind. You haven't minded since the moment I made the mistake of agreeing to let you show me to Malloy's. Now I don't have a lot of time here, so how about you just tell me where the damn office is."

Somehow, Kyle mustered up the gall to look offended at Clint's words. "Mister Adams, I was just trying to help you as best I could. And just so you know, you mentioned that you don't have a lot of time at least three or four—"

"Kyle," Clint said. "Before you finish what you were about to say, just tell me what I want to know before I take a swing at you myself."

Kyle started to say something, but managed to keep his tongue in check before anything else slipped out of his mouth. He raised his finger and pointed toward a lonely storefront situated at the corner of a busy intersection. There was no sign hanging over the front window or even anything painted upon the glass. There appeared to be a shingle hanging next to the door, but Clint couldn't read it from where he was standing.

Clint began walking toward the office. "Thank you," he said over his shoulder once he was certain that Kyle wasn't following behind like a puppy.

The street was indeed very busy, especially since it was early afternoon and many people were out and about conducting their business or making their way to one of a dozen stores in the immediate vicinity. It seemed the closer he got to the corner of Second and Timber Avenues, the more carriages rumbled down the street around him and the thicker the crowds got along the boardwalk.

Knowing full well that more of Malloy's men might be closing in on him at any moment, Clint kept his eyes searching the street. He looked for a face that had turned his way one too many times or a figure standing still amid all the movement. He even paid attention to the wagons that rolled by just in case they were going to stop too close to where he was standing.

But there was nothing that caught his eye and nobody standing in his way. In fact, no matter how thick the crowds were, they seemed to be steering clear of Malloy's office as though they were afraid to step too close to its unmarked walls.

Taking a quick glance behind him, Clint instantly spotted the figure standing across the street watching him. Annoyed, Clint shot Kyle a warning glare and knocked on Malloy's door.

TWENTY-TWO

In the space of a few seconds, the door came open and an almost painfully thin man took a step outside. His eyes were so sunken that they looked as though something inside the man's head was reeling them in. His skin hung on him like an ill-fitting suit. At first, the man's expression was completely blank. But as soon as he got a look at Clint, his eyes grew wide and what little color was left in his cheeks drained completely away.

"What do you want?" Jorgenson asked.

"I want to see Malloy. Judging by the look of you, I'd say that you either already know who I am or your boss likes to keep at least one ghost on his payroll."

Shifting nervously on his feet, Jorgenson looked behind him and then back at Clint. "Wait here," he said as he began shutting the door.

Clint kicked his foot against the bottom of the door and pushed it out of the way with a solid fist. Locking eyes with the thin man, he forced Jorgenson back into the building by walking steadily inside as though he fully intended to roll right over him.

Before he was knocked aside, Jorgenson stepped back and let Clint pass. "Mister Malloy," he shouted. "There's someone here to see you."

"Ah, Mister Adams," Malloy boomed from the next

room. "I was just sitting here thinking about how nice it would be to see you in person."

By the time Clint walked into the back room where Malloy's desk was situated, he could feel the blood pumping through his veins and his heart thumping inside his chest. The smug expression on the fat man's face did nothing to settle Clint's temper. "You know why I'm here, Malloy."

There was a pair of high-backed, cushioned chairs in front of Malloy's desk. When Clint first saw them, he thought they were both empty. But as soon as he was out of the small foyer, a figure got up from the chair on the left and reached out to grab a battered felt bowler that had been sitting on Malloy's desk.

Clint didn't recognize the man who tapped the bowler down onto his head. In fact, the other man looked nervous and almost subservient to the overbearing man behind the desk. The smaller figure turned to face Clint and held out his hand, a friendly smile etched across his face.

"Pleased to meet you, sir," the slender man said. "Are you a friend of Mister Malloy's?"

"Actually," Clint replied, "I'm here on business. So if you don't mind, I'd like a moment with him alone."

Although he looked disappointed, the man in the bowler retracted his hand and slid it into the pocket of his plain brown duster. "Of course." As he moved around the chair and past Clint, Krackow grunted and wheezed like an old man who was moving a bit faster than he should. Finally, he moved into the next room.

"Friend of yours?" Clint asked. "Or just another one of the locals who you've trained to bow down to you?"

Malloy laughed and sat down behind his desk. A man perfectly at ease and within his element, he opened one of his drawers and pulled out a box of cigars. He took his time in selecting one, biting off the end, and then holding it over a match. "He's an associate of mine."

"Did you get the offer I sent back with your men?" Clint asked. "Or did they even get a chance to tell you about it before you sent them back out to gun us down?"

"First of all, let me apologize for the way my men treated you. Believe me when I say that it wasn't you they were after." Malloy paused to take a long pull off his cigar. He offered one to Clint and after he was refused, put the box away. "I did get your offer. Unfortunately, I didn't get much of a chance to think it over before my men decided to take matters into their own hands. I assure you, I was most upset by the whole thing."

"I'm sure you were." Leaning forward, Clint put both hands on top of the desktop and stared down into Malloy's smug face. The sheen of sweat glistened off the large bald spot on top of the fat man's head. Clint couldn't tell if the other man was perspiring due to stress or if he was just always that slippery. Deciding on the latter, he tried not to breathe through his nose and went on. "Rayburn is gone. I was offering to compensate you for the loss simply because I'd come into some money recently and didn't want to take part in any violence if at all possible. Now that you've forced my hand, my advice is to just let him and his family go before anyone else gets hurt."

Smiling, Malloy said, "How generous of you. But I have an offer of my own." With the cigar clamped between his teeth, the fat man looked up at Clint with a deadly glint in his eyes. "You tell me right now where Rayburn is and then walk out of my office. You can stay in Brookins all you want and I'll even let you come to the fights for free. And just because I'm feeling good right now, I'll also throw in a little something extra." Malloy flicked his ashes onto the floor and blew a stream of smoke into Clint's face. "Your life."

Clint had met plenty of men like Malloy and he was all too familiar with what made them tick. There were only two things that those kind wanted: money and power. Only by threatening one of those two things could Clint hope to make someone like Malloy back down. Not even a gun in the fat man's face would have done any good. Not unless he pulled the trigger, that is.

Smiling more out of pity than amusement, Clint straightened up and shook his head. "Men like you would almost be funny if you weren't so damned pathetic. Since you won't listen to reason, perhaps you'll listen to this. Keep yourself and all your men away from Rayburn and his family. If they come up against me, I'll have no choice but to send them back to you in a pine box.

"You know who I am, so you also know that I can back up what I'm telling you right now. All you have to do is just sit back and try to run a square business for a change and this problem will go away. But if you keep starting trouble like you did the other night, I'll keep putting an end to that trouble . . ." Clint reached out and snatched the cigar straight out of Malloy's mouth and stubbed it out on the polished wood of the desktop. ". . . just like I did the other night."

For the first time since Clint had walked into that office, Malloy looked as though he was truly about to lose his temper. The fat man's face began to twitch and his eyes narrowed to thin slits. Clint stayed right where he was, glaring down at him as if daring him to make a move.

Although Malloy might have been angry, he wasn't necessarily stupid. For a few seconds, the two men locked in a silent battle of wills until finally Clint backed off and flicked the cigar stub onto the floor.

Clint dusted the stray bits of tobacco off his hand and said, "As much as I'd like to stay here and continue this lovely conversation, I've got some other business to attend to. If you were a smart man, this would be the last time we met. But unfortunately, I doubt that's the case."

Malloy was too angry to say a word. He knew that if he opened his mouth and allowed the words to start flowing, they wouldn't stop until he had his hands wrapped around Clint's throat. But then he saw something that put his mind at ease. As soon as he spotted it, the tension that had been boiling inside of him turned to vapor and disappeared.

Standing behind Clint, waiting there like just another part of the wall or even a stray piece of furniture, was Lawrence Krackow. Malloy didn't know when the killer had snuck back into the office, but he stood there as if he'd been waiting there for hours. When Clint turned around, he nearly ran into the gaunt figure.

The last Clint had seen of that man, he'd been excusing himself from the office. Now, like a wraith hiding out in half a shadow, he was back again. The second his eyes met Krackow's, the killer turned away as if he'd been scorned. Clint didn't like the fact that he hadn't heard Krackow come back into the room, but the man in the dented bowler seemed so skittish and frail that he hardly seemed like much of a threat at all. And since this man hadn't so much as looked at him the wrong way, Clint decided to keep walking.

"Excuse me again," Krackow said to Clint's back.

Ignoring the words, Clint threw open the front door and stormed out of the office.

"So," Malloy said after Krackow had settled back into his seat. "Was that really Clint Adams?"

"Most definitely."

"Do you still want this job?"

Reaching out with a cold, bony hand, Krackow picked up the whiskey glass that he'd emptied a few minutes ago. Running his tongue along the edge, he took in the few remaining drops of alcohol that had clung to its surface. After the glass was cleaned, he set it down and averted his eyes from Malloy's.

"Of course I want the job," Krackow said. "He'll be a lot of fun."

"Good, because for the moment, he's all you need to worry about."

"But what about that other fighter?" Krackow asked, looking mildly disappointed. "And his family?"

"I've had men tracking him since he left town earlier this morning. Once you're done with Adams, you can go and mop up whoever is left. There's others who seem to be getting some ideas about crossing me as well and they all need to be dealt with." Malloy opened his drawer and took out another cigar. When he chewed off the end, he imagined it was Clint's head he was biting off. The flame of the match became a fire that consumed all of those who made the mistake of thinking they could pull one over on him.

"Trust me," Malloy said. "There won't be a shortage of bodies for you to play with."

TWENTY-THREE

"How'd it go?"

Those three words hit Clint dead in the face the instant his boots hit the boardwalk outside of Malloy's building. They chewed like little daggers into his ears and they came from Kyle's mouth in a quicker succession than any of his punches the night before.

"Don't you have anything else to do right now?" Clint asked as he passed by Kyle and kept right on walking.

"Like it or not, I'm in this," Kyle said, following one step behind Clint. "I been in it since I told Malloy to go to hell and beat the tar outta that man last week. He knows he ain't the boss of every man. Especially not me. Yessir, especially not me!"

"And I suppose last night was another of your little rebellions, huh? Let me guess, you were supposed to win that one and you told Malloy to go to hell by taking a haymaker right on the chin, which nearly took your head off."

Kyle didn't have much of an answer for that one and Clint enjoyed the silence that followed. He savored it all the way back to Sal's where he untied Eclipse's reins from the hitching post in front of the saloon. Before getting in the saddle, Clint turned on the young boxer and said, "Thanks for showing me around town, Kyle. I really do appreciate it. Now if you want some good advice, I'll give it to you." He swung up onto the stallion's back and turned to face the western edge of town. "Find a place to hide before things really get bad, because it's coming sooner than you think."

Kyle strode up next to Clint, puffing his chest out as though he was getting ready for a shot at the title. "Don't you worry about me none. I seen enough men tryin' to do me harm than you could—"

A shot cracked in the air, causing Clint to reflexively duck down low and go for his gun. He could hear a bullet whipping toward him and then the sickening sound of lead slapping against flesh, carving its way through bone. The next thing he knew, Clint was blinded by a wave of blood which sprayed across his face.

Clint dropped down from Eclipse's back and landed in a crouch with the stallion between himself and the direction of the gunshot. At the same time his feet hit the dirt, Kyle's body dropped face first onto the ground to reveal a small hole in the back of his head.

Keeping his head down low, Clint hurried out from behind his horse, searching the area for any sign of whoever had taken that shot. The street was crowded with people of all ages caught in the middle of their daily routines. As the gunshot echoed in the air, those people scattered in every direction, not giving him the slightest clue as to where he should look.

For a second, Clint swore he could see a small wisp of smoke hovering over head level and dispersing into the slowly moving wind. Although that would have been a direct line between the cloud and Kyle, there was nobody else standing there at the moment. What few people Clint could see were ducking into stores or hurrying away down the street.

"Damn," Clint whispered.

Krackow was damn proud of that shot. Taken from the hip, it had come after pulling the gun from his coat pocket and aiming for no more than about a second and a half. He'd stood amid the people shuffling down the boardwalk for a little while, patiently waiting for that one perfect moment when nobody was looking directly at him and his target was still in position.

He'd fired once, pocketed the gun again and then scrambled off with the rest of the crowd, wearing a mask of surprised shock matching the expressions of nearly everyone else in the vicinity. Everyone except for Adams, that is. Krackow couldn't help but admire the speed with which Adams ducked for cover and got ready to return fire. It wasn't often that he got to see someone like that in action.

Most of the time, he found taking someone's life was so easy that it bordered on pathetic. That was why he needed to make things interesting for himself and why he would never turn away the hard jobs. Clint Adams would have been the type of assignment that most men in Krackow's field would have passed on. And as he scurried away with the rest of the frightened sheep, Krackow made sure to keep his body turned so that he could watch Clint out of the corner of his eye.

The Gunsmith was moving swiftly behind posts and water troughs, ready for the next shot to come and watching for anyone nearby who might be the one to fire it. His eyes had the hard glint of a hawk's and the way he moved was purely predatory.

Krackow had no doubt that if he revealed himself at that moment, he wouldn't have been alive to see the next. For now, his job was done. That boxer was on Malloy's list of expendable talent, which meant that the killer was already three hundred dollars richer. The big money would come later, once Clint Adams was running for his life and taking his last breaths.

Smiling to himself now that he'd tagged along with a panicked group of locals far enough to turn the corner, Krackow slowed his pace and headed for a brothel on Fourth Avenue. He was in the mood to celebrate.

TWENTY-FOUR

Kneeling down next to Kyle's body, Clint checked the fighter over to see if there was anything he could do for him. Unfortunately, the bullet that had gone through Kyle's mind had done more than enough. Clint knew that Malloy was behind this, but there was nobody in the area besides himself and the dead man.

What bothered him more than anything else was the fact that he hadn't seen the shot coming. There'd been no shouted threats or even a break in the flow of people walking down the boardwalk. All Clint had seen was Kyle standing in front of him, and then a spray of blood across his eyes.

Thinking about that, Clint stood up and touched a hand to his face. There was still a sticky layer of blood on his skin. He quickly wiped his face off as best as he could after holstering his gun and checking the street one more time. There wasn't anything left to do here besides get Kyle out of the street. The best he could do was remove the dead man's jacket and use it to cover his upper body and face.

Clint knew that whoever had taken that shot was probably long gone by now. Hopping back onto Eclipse, Clint snapped the reins and charged for the western path out of town. He figured that Malloy was probably going to send more of his men after Rayburn since the boxer was relatively unprotected. Clint just hoped that Malloy didn't know exactly where Rayburn was going because if he did, he would surely be there by now.

Visions of finding Rayburn's body lying next to Danny and Myra haunted Clint's mind from the moment Eclipse broke into a run and charged for the edge of town. As the Darley Arabian's hooves pounded against the cold, packed earth, Clint kept his eyes searching high and low, back and forth, looking for any trace of another gunman.

His mind flashed through the memory of Kyle's final moments, hoping to find anything he might have missed the first time around—a face in the crowd, a familiar voice, even the sound of the shot itself, anything that would give him a clue of what to look for when that killer struck again.

Eclipse raced out of Brookins and tore down the westward trail, heading toward the mountains. The more Clint thought about what had happened, the worse he felt for not being able to do a damn thing to save Kyle. Suddenly, it seemed as if someone else had been taken in by the reputation of the Gunsmith. It was someone he never would have thought capable of such a thing: himself.

Figuring that just standing there next to Kyle would have been enough to protect the fighter from any harm, Clint had let his guard down and gotten a man killed. He'd given the killer a free shot and then left Kyle dead in the street. Rather than dwell too long on those thoughts, Clint leaned down close to the stallion's back and searched even harder for an ambush.

If he couldn't save Kyle, then by god he wasn't about to let Rayburn and the others down as well.

Although Eclipse was tearing down the trail faster than most horses could ever hope to run, Clint felt as though the ride was taking forever. Every step of the way, Clint's eyes were scanning the horizon and searching every bit of his surroundings like a starving hawk desperate to spot even the slightest bit of movement in a stretch of fields that went on for miles in every direction.

Finally, as Eclipse rounded a bend in the trail, there was a glint of something metallic catching the afternoon sun. Clint pulled on the reins to slow the stallion down. He was facing a small break in the trail, which headed into the tree line and then up the side of a mountain. Although he wasn't familiar with this territory, Clint figured the smaller trail was a path that probably skirted the mountain itself and might even lead up into a mining or logging settlement.

He couldn't say which one was the case, or even if either were true. But after what had happened to Kyle, he didn't want to leave anything else to chance. Eclipse seemed eager to run again and shifted anxiously on his feet.

"Easy, boy," he whispered as he stared at the mountainside.

Just as he was about to head back down the trail and forget about the flicker he'd seen, Clint spotted the same thing again. Coming from a spot just inside a stretch of pines, the glint was definitely a reflection off of metal or even glass. Either way, Clint was certain that it came from other men working their way along that ridge.

Turning Eclipse toward the break in the trail, Clint made sure to keep the stallion from taking off at a full run. Now that he knew where the flicker had come from, it was easier to spot it again. As soon as he caught the slightest glimpse of figures up ahead of him, Clint pulled Eclipse to a stop and eased himself out of the saddle. Without taking his eyes from the trail ahead of him, Clint reached around to grab the rifle hanging from the stallion's side and slid in a few cartridges.

"Stay quiet, now," he whispered to the horse as he pat its neck. "I'll be back for you in a minute."

Clint didn't have to look back to know the horse wasn't about to move more than a few steps from where he'd left him. The trail was thinner here and even on foot, Clint was having a hard time moving forward without stepping on too many fallen branches or slipping on loose rocks.

From what he could see, there were two men up ahead. Since he'd gained on them so quickly, Clint figured they were either staying in position or moving very slowly. As he got closer, he could tell that both men had their backs to him and were looking down on the trail below. One of them was sighting down the barrel of a rifle.

Clint stepped off the trail and headed up the gentle slope where the trees got bigger and closer together. He maneuvered straight up the slope until he was in a position that put him a little higher and just behind the other two men. Clint then crouched down low with the rifle set across his knees and edged forward just enough so he could get a good look over the men's shoulders and down onto the main trail. He couldn't see much, but he could see enough of the battered wagon to know it was the one belonging to Rayburn and his family.

Looking back to the men on the ridge, Clint could see that both men wore gun belts around their waists. The one with the rifle was lying flat on his belly, taking his sweet time as though he was about to pick off a slow buffalo from the rest of the herd. That man's partner was down on one knee, keeping watch on the rest of the area. Every so often, he would take a quick glance over his shoulder. Although he was looking back toward where Eclipse was waiting, the man didn't seem to be worrying about the higher ground.

All the better, Clint thought as he slowly brought the rifle up to his shoulder and sighted down the barrel.

TWENTY-FIVE

"Damnit," Rayburn cursed as he took one more swing at the wagon with his hammer.

The hammer glanced off of one of the wagon's wheels and slammed into the side with all the force of the fighter's muscles behind it. Rayburn had been trying to pound the wheel's metal rim back into place so that he could get moving again. But since he was a much better boxer than he was a carpenter, the hammer never quite seemed to land where he wanted it.

After taking another swing, which took a chunk out of the bottom edge of the wagon's body, Rayburn stood up, cocked his arm back, and pitched the hammer into the air as though the thing had burned his hand. This time, the tool landed exactly where he'd wanted it. Unfortunately, it was about thirty feet down the road.

"What's the matter, Ed?" Myra asked from the back of the wagon. "Do you need any help?"

Rayburn pressed his hands against his head and kicked the wagon wheel in frustration. That, more than anything else he'd done in the last half hour, seemed to do the most good for the wheel's rim since it had started to come loose an hour ago. When his boot made contact with the metal, it knocked the rim partly back into place.

Myra stuck her head around the wagon to check on her

brother. "Did you do any permanent damage yet?" she asked.

Sitting on the driver's seat, Danny started giggling and then quickly put a hand to his mouth to try and keep the noise down.

"I'm glad all of you find this so damn funny," Rayburn said as he began stomping down the road toward his hammer. "Because we're losing daylight by sitting still like this and we need to put as much space between us and that town as possible."

Myra hopped down out of the wagon and ran to fetch the hammer. After picking it up and jogging back, she put it into Rayburn's hand. "Can you fix it, Ed?" she asked. "And don't say yes just to make us feel better."

Gripping the hammer in a tight fist, Rayburn walked back to the damaged wagon wheel and gave it another kick with all the strength he could muster. Surprisingly enough, the rim was nearly set back into place. Rayburn tossed the hammer into the wagon and looked up with a satisfied grin on his face.

Just as he was about to give the wheel another kick, something caught Rayburn's attention. First, he heard it and then he saw it. There was movement coming from farther back on the trail.

Sounded like footsteps.

Looked like two men on horseback.

"Need some help?" the first one asked. He was wearing a dark gray coat that might have been something left over from the war. His hands were covered in black leather gloves and polished steel winked with reflected sunlight from the tips of his boots.

The man's name was Faraday. Rayburn recognized him as one of Malloy's and he didn't have to see the holster under that gray coat to know full well it was there.

The man riding next to Faraday must have worked for Malloy as well, but Rayburn had never seen him before. This other one looked like an Indian, with dark skin the color of rusted steel. The poncho he wore looked like a horse's blanket and the legs coming from the bottom of it were covered in well-worn chaps. When the Indian turned to get a better look at Myra, he exposed a thick scar that ran across the front of his neck.

Rayburn forced a friendly smile onto his face and hoped that Faraday didn't know that he'd been recognized. "Actually," the fighter said, "I think I managed to get this damn thing back together again. It wasn't much. Just a wobbly rim that was fixin' to come off. Looks like it's fine now, but thanks all the same."

After a quick look to his partner, Faraday swung down from his saddle and started walking toward the wagon. He was about ten yards away. "Where you folks headed?" he asked.

Trying to act as casual as possible, Rayburn walked toward the back of the wagon to stand in front of Myra. He also reached in and got the hammer. "Headed south to visit some relatives," Rayburn said. "Cousin of mine took sick and needs some help fixing up his place. Just mending fences and such."

Danny hopped down from the driver's seat and landed with a crunch of boots on gravel. The sound caused Rayburn to flinch and look back with a fierce, silent order to stay where he was.

Both of Malloy's men were walking closer, leading their horses by the reins. They were about five yards away.

"I'd hate to see you and that pretty lady of yours get stuck," Faraday said. "Why don't you let us take them passengers on back into town. After my partner here gets your wagon fixed up, you can drive it back and get a new wheel. After all, the land gets awful rough awful quick in these parts."

Rayburn turned and gave Myra a nod and looked quickly to the inside of the wagon. She understood him perfectly and hopped up inside, motioning for Danny to follow. Once both of them were tucked away, Rayburn planted his feet and squared his shoulders, the hammer slung over his shoulder.

"Thanks again," Rayburn said. "But I've fixed this old wheel. You can move along."

Faraday stopped about ten feet in front of the fighter, a smug look plastered across his finely chiseled features. "Wait a minute . . . I know who you are. You're that boxer that dropped Calhoun the other night."

After letting go of his horse's reins, the Indian kept walking past Faraday and headed straight toward the wagon.

"I heard Calhoun's aching for a rematch," Faraday continued. "Too bad he won't get one."

TWENTY-SIX

Faraday swept open his coat and reached for the gun strapped to his leg. As soon as his hand touched the handle, the Indian broke into a run.

Feeling a little more in his element, Rayburn braced himself in a solid fighting stance and swung the hammer straight down and out. The muscles in his bulky arm pulled with all their might, moving the hammer as if it was nothing more than a stick being tossed onto a bonfire. Praying that his aim was true, the fighter pushed his muscles just a little bit harder the last second before letting go.

The hammer turned awkwardly in the air one time before the blunt metal end caught Faraday square in the chest right below the neck. The impact took Faraday off his feet and knocked him straight back as though he'd been tied to a runaway horse. His gun went off, but sent its round into the soil as his arms flailed instinctively to break his fall.

In Rayburn's mind, everything began to flow as if he was in the ring. His vision narrowed down to absorb everything that was happening within his arm's reach and his instincts were ready to alert him of attacks coming from any side. His head thrummed in time to his racing pulse and his ears were still ringing from the gunshot that had gone off like a cannon in front of him.

Before he could turn to look for the Indian, Rayburn felt something hit him with all the force of a mule's kick. The fighter's ribs were suddenly ablaze with pain and all the wind was knocked from his lungs. As he started falling, Rayburn felt the Indian's arm wrapped around his midsection and his shoulder driving him back.

Having thrown his entire body into a running tackle, the Indian landed on top of Rayburn. When they both hit the ground, neither man was able to get enough leverage to throw a punch. The Indian, however, was more prepared for the landing and sent his forehead crashing down onto the bridge of Rayburn's nose with a heavy *thump*.

Searing bolts of raw agony exploded from Rayburn's nose and lanced all the way through to the back of his skull. He'd had his nose broken plenty of times, but that still didn't make the experience any less painful. His vision started to darken and blur. Hot tears burned in his eyes and a cold fury formed at the pit of his stomach.

When Rayburn struck back, he did so without being able to see his target as anything more than a moving blur. As his arm came around, he twisted his body along with it and didn't stop until his fist slammed against something solid.

Whatever he'd hit, Rayburn felt it topple over to the side and land next to him. The fighter reached out and grabbed a fistful of what felt like some kind of woven material, using his hold to pull the rest of his body up into a kneeling position. By the time he was upright, Rayburn was looking down at the Indian through a haze of bloody mist and bright lights dancing across his field of vision.

The blood that ran into Rayburn's mouth tasted like hot, rusty soup. Every breath he took was like inhaling burning ash. As soon as he gathered up his strength, Rayburn lashed out with a fist that slammed into the Indian's face, snapped his head back and bounced it off the frozen ground.

The Indian was pounded again and again until the only thing holding him up was Rayburn's grip on his poncho.

When the fighter finally let go and allowed the Indian to drop, he knew that the trouble wasn't over yet. Something in the back of his mind, the very instinct that allowed him to survive inside the ring, told him he needed to get to his feet and finish what he'd begun.

Climbing to his feet, Rayburn felt his entire world teeter precariously one way and then shift beneath him all the way in the opposite direction. The pain from his broken nose was like a fire inside of him, urging him to move faster. But the harder he tried, the shakier he felt. By the time Rayburn was standing, he wobbled like a drunk, grabbing hold of the side of the wagon for support.

The first thing he looked for was Myra.

Although Rayburn couldn't quite make out any details through the fog drifting behind his eyes, he could see the color of her coat and the blonde of her hair. She reached out for him and said something he couldn't quite make out.

Ignoring his sister's words, Rayburn staggered around to face the place where Faraday had been standing. Every instinct inside of him was screaming for him to hurry up and turn around. His body moved as fast as he could, but still it didn't feel fast enough.

Finally, he managed to fight through the pain and get himself ready for another round. What he found when he was looking in the right direction was just another blob, this one in the vague shape of a man covered in gray.

The blurred figure moved and held something out toward him.

"Tell her goodbye, you big dumb bastard," came Faraday's voice through the haze.

All Rayburn heard after that was a gunshot and Myra's voice.

She was screaming.

TWENTY-SEVEN

Clint knew one of the first mistakes someone could make when lining up a rifle shot was thinking about it too hard. As he drew a bead on the shooter taking aim below him, Clint thought about what had happened back in town and whether or not it had been these two who'd shot Kyle in the street outside of Sal's.

Although Clint knew better than to let himself be distracted from his shot, he'd been diverted just long enough to only hear the steps coming up behind him when it was almost too late to do anything about it. *Almost*, however, wasn't enough to save the poor fool who tried to sneak up on Clint.

Clint's ears picked up a rustle of leaves that was too sharp and too quick to have been caused by a turn of the wind. And when his survival instincts told him there were eyes boring into the back of his head, Clint spun around just in time to see a scrawny, pale-skinned kid no more than eighteen years old pouncing toward him clutching a Bowie knife that was roughly the same size as his own forearm.

With a mixture of fearlessness and stupidity, the kid ducked low and threw himself toward Clint with the huge blade leading the way. The sharp piece of steel cut through the air and glinted in the sunlight, shaving off a strip of Clint's jacket and shirt, raking along the flesh underneath. Smiling victoriously, the kid made the mistake in thinking that he'd already won the scuffle when it had only just begun.

Clint managed to twist his body to avoid most of the blade that would have buried itself deep into his stomach otherwise. A sharp pain accompanied the sound of ripping fabric, but wasn't enough to worry about. Although he could feel the knife cut him and the blood start to flow, he knew it wasn't more than a scratch. What he really had to worry about was all the other men who now knew exactly where he was and what he was doing. The element of surprise was gone and that was the big loss.

Gripping the rifle in one hand, Clint locked his fist around the kid's wrist before he could pull his knife back and do a hell of a lot more damage. Clint twisted the guy's wrist, pulled it forward and held on tight. He then turned his entire body around in a tight circle, bending the attacker's wrist the wrong way until the knife finally came loose and dropped to the ground beneath him.

"Son of a bitch," grunted one of the men on the ridge below Clint's position.

In one swift motion, Clint spun back around with his elbow raised and caught the other man with a crushing blow to the jaw. He kept turning and swept his elbow all the way around as though he was trying to take the guy's head clean off his shoulders. The attacker's head snapped back and he dropped back into the bushes alongside the narrow trail.

Clint didn't have to see the other two men to know what he needed to do next. Holding on tight to his rifle, he dropped straight down to the ground and began rolling to his left. As soon as his chest hit the dirt, he heard the first shot ring out as a mound of dirt was kicked up less than a few inches from his right side.

At the sound of the gunshot rolling down from the nearby mountainside, both Rayburn and Faraday turned to look in that direction. Knowing an opportunity when he saw one, Rayburn ducked his head down low and dashed toward the Indian's unmoving body.

Faraday had only been distracted for about a second and a half and when he turned back to take his shot at the boxer, Rayburn was already on the move. Cursing, Faraday pulled his trigger while trying to track the boxer's movement with his pistol. The bullet went high and slammed into the back of the battered old wagon.

Rayburn fought back the panic that was creeping into his whole body with all the instincts that had kept him from losing his head when facing another man in the ring. Although this was nothing like a bare-knuckle slugfest, Rayburn found it was the same will to survive that kept him moving even as Faraday took another shot at him.

This time, the bullet tore a painful chunk out of the back of Rayburn's thigh. Feeling as though his muscles had suddenly caught on fire, Rayburn ignored the pain and got himself to keep moving forward. He was just able to reach down and grab the Indian by the front of his poncho.

Although the Indian was a fairly big man, it didn't even take all of Rayburn's strength to lift the unconscious man up off the ground and drag him along. All the hairs along the back of the fighter's neck stood on end, warning him somehow that another bullet was about to tear into his flesh. Just when he'd thought his time was up, Rayburn twisted his body around and threw himself to the ground, making sure to pull the Indian on top of him.

All Rayburn could see before the Indian blocked his vision was Faraday's cold eyes staring back at him, a cloud of smoke swirling around his face. The pistol fired again, echoing like thunder down the mountain trail as another round of gunshots came from above.

The bullet slammed into the Indian's back and plowed through his entire body. After bouncing off of enough bones and internal organs, the piece of lead came out through the Indian's rib cage, creasing Rayburn's side as it went. That was enough to wake the Indian up, who began struggling in Rayburn's grasp like a fish who just realized it had been hooked.

Clenching his teeth and growling like an enraged animal, Rayburn barely even realized he'd been shot again as he cocked both arms back and tightened his grip on the dying man's collar. With all his might, he pushed the body away from him and launched it toward Faraday just as the man in gray squeezed off another shot.

Before the shooting had started, Faraday thought everything was well in hand. Now, he wasn't sure if his partner was conscious or just being yanked around like a rag doll. The others up on the ridge should have had him covered, but now they were shooting at themselves. And now, the Indian was flying toward him, covered in blood and staring at him with blank, unseeing eyes.

Faraday fired his pistol again, this time sending a wild shot into the Indian's chest. But that didn't stop the body from coming. Instead, the impact of the bullet twisted the Indian around just enough so that his shoulder smashed into Faraday's body and sent him reeling backward away from the wagon.

Rayburn stood hunched over, waiting for round two as the pain from his fresh wounds began to seep into his system. His body leaned to one side as his wounded leg threatened to buckle under his weight and then he leaned even farther as the shallow tear in his back began to flare up.

He watched to make sure that his plan had worked and actually felt a rush of excitement when he saw Faraday get taken off his feet by the body that had been tossed at him. Rayburn turned to make sure that Myra and Danny were all right when something caught his attention. Lying on the ground, where it must have been dropped by the Indian, was a small pistol. Picking it up as he walked toward the wagon, Rayburn tightened his fist around the grip and thumbed back the hammer without even thinking about it.

Myra's screaming had stopped, which somehow frightened Rayburn more than if she'd still been carrying on. When he poked his head around the wagon, he saw nothing but the pair of restless horses straining against their reins, scared senseless by all the loud noises.

"You back here, Myra?" Rayburn asked as he stepped around the horses and looked from side to side.

Even though he was hoping to find her, Rayburn nearly took a shot at his sister when she burst out from underneath the wagon and ran toward him with arms outstretched.

"Oh thank god," she said in a sobbing voice. "I heard all the shooting and thought for sure you'd been killed."

Rayburn wrapped his arms around her and held her tight. "Are you all right?" he asked.

Nodding, she buried her face in his shirt and turned just enough so her voice could be heard. "I didn't want to leave you, but I didn't want to get in the way in case something happened. I tried to get the team moving, but they were too spooked to do much of anything, so I hid and waited for you."

"It's all right now. Where's Danny?"

"I think he's still under the wagon. Should I get him?"

In the blink of an eye, Rayburn went from feeling joyous relief to cold terror.

Faraday stepped around the side of the wagon, holding his gun in one hand and Danny in the other. The front of his coat was smeared with the Indian's blood and the smile on his face had a crazy tilt to it. Without saying a single word, he raised his gun and pointed it at Rayburn. Then, when he had the fighter's attention, he turned and placed the barrel against Danny's temple.

TWENTY-EIGHT

Once he came to a rest, Clint found himself lying in the middle of the main trail leading up the ridge, on his back with the rifle clutched against his chest. He could feel the earth pounding beneath his entire body as one of the men came running toward him.

The man rushing forward thought he had plenty of time to get up close, put his pistol up against Clint's head, and blow his brains out. When he saw Clint bring his rifle around, however, it was too late for him to come up with another course of action.

Ignoring the fact that his target was upside-down, Clint brought the rifle up to his eye, took aim, and squeezed the trigger.

First there was the puff of smoke and then came the crack of a shot. After that, the man couldn't hear a thing but the pained grunt that came from the back of his throat once lead slammed through his chest and out his back. Everything went black as his body toppled backward. He was dead by the time his back hit the gravelly soil.

After dropping his target with one shot, Clint kept right on rolling until he was back in the cover of bushes. Bare, frozen branches stabbed into his sides and more than one tore into the bloody cut in his side.

It was instinct more than anything else that caused Clint

to put his leg out and stop his movement. It was Clint's momentum that kept him sliding in the same direction, nearly pitching him off the side of the ridge and down the base of the mountain. Reflexively, he threw his arms out with the rifle gripped between them and managed to snag one of the larger bushes at its base, which stopped him less than an inch before he'd rolled completely off the ridge.

Another gunshot cracked through the air. This time, it was a rifle and since no lead flew in his direction, Clint knew that the shooter he'd spotted had just taken a shot at Rayburn's wagon down below. Using his hold on the rifle to gain some leverage, Clint pulled himself back onto more level ground and got his feet beneath him. He was careful to keep his head low as he rushed toward the shooter's position.

Once he was upright again, Clint had no trouble spotting the man with the rifle. Now up on one knee, the shooter levered in another round and took a quick look over his shoulder.

"Mike, did you get that bast—" the shooter started to say before he caught sight of the dead body. "Aww, shit," was all he could get out as he wheeled around to face Clint, who was now charging at him full force.

Clint readied his own rifle to take his next shot, but wasn't able to do so before the shooter turned on him for a point-blank shot. There was less than two feet separating both men when the shooter's finger began tensing on his trigger. Knowing he'd almost run out of time, Clint adjusted his grip on the rifle stock and swung it like a club with all the force he could muster.

The barrel of Clint's rifle sailed through the air and connected with the shooter's hand right where it was gripping his own gun's stock. Three of the shooter's fingers broke on contact, turning into bone-splintered mush beneath the crushing steel. Howling in pain, the shooter managed to pull his trigger.

Clint knew that following through with his swing was

going to be more important than the damage it did, since it was the rest of his rifle's motion that knocked the shooter's gun off target. The rifle went off, but fortunately it was pointed toward the sky and the bullet sailed toward the clouds with a deafening explosion.

Continuing with his swinging motion, Clint swept the gun out and back until the butt of its stock was pointed toward the shooter's gut. That was precisely where Clint hit him when he jabbed with the wooden stock and knocked all of the breath from the shooter's lungs. Clint took a step back and let the shooter drop to his knees before sending one of his boots into the other man's face.

The shooter's mouth and nose were suddenly awash in blood. When he slumped down to the ground, the gunman looked all but dead.

Clint rushed forward to get a look at the man he'd just dropped, kicking the rifle out of his reach as he went. Although he was no doctor, Clint could tell that the man was at least going to live to see another day. How long it would be before he woke up, on the other hand, was another matter altogether.

After checking on the kid who'd had the knife to make sure that one was still out cold, Clint looked down onto the trail below. With his ears still ringing from the gunshots going off at such close range, he'd been unable to hear much of anything else. As soon as he peeked over the ridge, however, he immediately saw the other two figures near Rayburn. One of them was on the ground at the boxer's feet while the other one held a gun pointed at Danny's head.

"Oh god," Clint said to himself.

As he brought the rifle up to his shoulder and quickly figured out his shot, Clint could hear something rustling through the bushes behind him. Knowing full well that it was probably the kid with the knife trying to shake off his pain and move in for an ambush, Clint didn't allow his mind to stray too far from its task of judging distance to his target, factor in the wind, and pick a spot to shoot for that wouldn't hit the boy if it missed.

Clint shifted his stance slightly, lowered his aim just a bit, and took in a breath as the shuffling behind him turned into footsteps heading his way. He then let his breath ease out and started gently squeezing the trigger, being careful not to let his motion pull the rifle in any direction.

Before the shot was fired, Clint spun around just in time to see the knife fighter rushing toward him with a smaller blade raised over his head.

Clint pushed his rifle forward as the kid with the knife ran straight into the extended barrel. Even as he saw what he'd done, the attacker stabbed downward with the blade while pressing himself harder against the rifle in an attempt to extend his reach enough to bury the sharpened steel into Clint's face.

Clint used the rifle to push the kid back as the knife slashed down. Every muscle in his back and arms strained with the effort and he felt pain lance through his shoulder as he nearly threw it out of its socket to keep from getting himself sliced open. The blade came so close that Clint could feel the edge of it tickle his brow as it whipped past him and his finger pulled back hard on the trigger.

When the rifle went off, there was only a muffled thumping, which sounded more like a stick of dynamite going off underwater than a gunshot. The kid's face was nearly pressed up against his own by this time and all Clint could see was the attacker's eyes clouding over as death swept him away. His jaw hung open and he let out his final breath, which trickled out of him like a slow leak.

Reminding himself that there was still plenty he needed to do, Clint swept the image of that kid's face to the back of his mind and shoved the twitching body away from him. By the time it landed, Clint was already looking back down onto the main trail and figuring out his next shot.

This time when he sighted down toward Rayburn's wagon, Clint couldn't get a clear shot at the man holding Danny. Then he saw the figure dressed in gray backing away from the wagon. Clint's eyes narrowed and he tried to concentrate on figuring out a perfect shot.

His first impulse was to take careful aim and pick off the gunman before he had a chance to hurt the boy. But no matter how steady Clint's hand was, it couldn't give him a clear enough shot.

The other man was holding Danny too damn close.

As much as Clint wanted to take his chances in order to save the boy, he wasn't about to let a gust of wind or a flinch in the wrong direction mess up his aim. From this distance, even the slightest miscalculation could cost Danny his life.

His finger tensed on the trigger and then relaxed again.

Blinking away a bead of sweat that had dripped into his eye, Clint decided to wait for the other man to step back and then decided to take the shot.

Either decision could kill the boy, but doing nothing would have the same result. Every time he made up his mind to act, he realized he would be making a mistake. All of Clint's indecision took place in the matter of seconds.

His mind raced, weighing his options and guessing at how much time he had before that man down there pulled his trigger.

"Damnit," he hissed while staring down that cold barrel.

TWENTY-NINE

"Why don't you let the woman go and die like a man?" Faraday asked with that murderous gleam in his eye.

Rayburn let go of his sister and moved her behind him. Once she saw what he was doing, Myra struggled and squirmed in an attempt to keep from being pushed aside.

Without taking his eyes off of Faraday, Rayburn told her, "Let me handle this. Go on now and hide beneath the front seat."

At first, Myra seemed just as confused as Faraday by those words. But then she quit trying to outmuscle her brother and reluctantly broke away. It was all she could do to keep from breaking down in hysterics, but she somehow managed to hold herself together as she ran around the other side of the wagon and climbed inside. The first place she went to was the back of the wagon.

From there, she thought about why her brother had told her to go under the front seat. There wasn't anything there but . . . the shotgun. Her heart skipped a beat and she reached forward in an attempt to reach beneath the seat from behind it. The only thing between her and that shotgun was the flimsy tarp and a dresser that was loaded just behind the driver's seat. Although that dresser was small, it had been loaded up with most of the family's clothes and even some valuables.

It had taken all three of them to load that thing inside the wagon, and now Myra tried to move it aside on her own. Every muscle in her arms and back worked until they felt like they were going to snap off of her bones. Agonizing heat swept through her shoulders as she kept trying to move that dresser without being too loud about it.

She knew if she could pull it forward or even rock it back and forth a few times, she might get it to budge. But that would have alerted the gunman as well, who would have in turn killed her son.

Hot tears streamed down her face as Myra did her best to move that damn dresser.

Standing next to the horses, Rayburn locked eyes with Faraday, only looking down once to get a look at Danny. "Did you hurt him?" the fighter asked.

"No," Faraday sneered. "I wanted to wait so's you could watch when that happened."

Standing there, watching the tears well up in Danny's eyes, Rayburn could feel his whole world spinning wildly around him. The light started to dim and his knees became shakier with every passing second. It was then that he could feel the blood as it seeped through his clothes and dripped down his skin. The wounds he'd taken must have been worse than he'd thought since they were flowing with no end in sight. The boxer knew he couldn't stand there and think straight for very long in his current condition.

"It's me that you want, isn't it?" Rayburn said.

Faraday looked down at the boy and then back at Rayburn. "Sure it is, but since you killed my partner, I figure that you owe me a little extra blood."

Myra pushed aside all the fear that was coursing through her mind and concentrated solely on the task at hand. Suddenly, she remembered something about that dresser. More importantly, she remembered something that was *inside* the dresser. Crawling on hands and knees inside the wagon, she reached around until she could pull open one of the left-hand drawers.

She did her best to be as quiet as possible, but the more she heard the men talk outside, the less time she knew her son had. Straining her arm until her shoulder was nearly jammed inside the heavy piece of furniture, Myra could just barely feel something in the back of the drawer with the tip of her middle finger.

It felt at first like a small part of a table leg or even a large piece of cork. But when she got a hold of the thing behind the dresser and pulled, Myra felt the thing coming loose as if it was sliding out of some sort of case. The thing wasn't very big, but getting it out of its holder nearly popped Myra's shoulder out of its socket. After it came loose, she managed to keep herself from dropping it as she pulled her arm back.

In her trembling fingers was a small dagger with a thick wooden handle that was covered in cork. The blade was chipped and rusted, but it seemed to still have enough of an edge to it. When she saw what she'd found, Myra felt strong again. Suddenly, she wasn't so helpless anymore and she crawled out of the wagon as fast she could to see what good she could do with her discovery.

She figured Rayburn would probably want her to get the blade to him, but there was no way to do that without walking right in front of the killer who had her son. Suddenly, another idea came to her and she dropped down close to the ground, hoping that she could pull it off before it was too late.

The rifle sat in Clint's hands, propped up by his bended knee. His body was so still it might have been carved out of the mountain itself. Finally, he decided that Danny would be just as dead if the gunman killed him or if Clint's bullet went astray. At least the boy had a chance if Clint fired first.

Still, knowing that didn't make the decision any easier.

All he needed was an opening. Nothing too big or fancy, but just something that would give him a clear shot. His mind screamed for him to just aim and fire, but something else held him back. Clint wasn't a big one on fate or divine guidance, but there was something keeping him from taking his shot.

Although he couldn't hear what was going on, he could tell from the way the man in gray was moving that something was about to happen.

Rayburn knew that he'd stalled the killer as long as he could. After all the years he'd spent in the ring, he could tell when his opponents were thinking and when they were just out for blood. Faraday was beyond thought now and had crossed over into that second category.

Looking around for Myra, he'd hoped that she'd at least gotten her hands on a weapon so that she could protect herself if she wound up dead. The Indian's pistol felt small and awkward in his hand, but Rayburn figured he'd have to use it. Even though Faraday's gun was already out and ready, Rayburn knew he'd have to take his chances while putting the life of his nephew in jeopardy.

Faraday took another step back and pressed the gun to Danny's head. "Hope yer watchin'," he sneered. "Because this is where I earn my extra share of Malloy's money!"

Pushing the gun to Danny's temple, Faraday made sure that he was looking only at Rayburn as he pressed the steel closer against the boy's head and began tightening his finger around the trigger.

Suddenly, blinding pain shot up from Faraday's ankle and his right leg folded completely in half beneath him. He knew he hadn't tripped over anything. It was just as though his leg decided to give up on him. As he began to topple over, he could still feel the pain, which was now so intense that his vision started to blur.

At the last second, he managed to hold himself upright and look down at the woman looking up at him from underneath the wagon. In her hand was a small dagger that was still covered in wet crimson. Blood poured out from the deep gash behind his ankle and looked as though it would never stop flowing out of him.

"You . . . you . . . bitch," Faraday said as he stumbled another step back and swung the pistol toward Myra.

Rayburn brought his own gun up as quick as he could, but Danny was still between him and the killer. Besides that, he wasn't sure if he could pull the trigger fast enough to keep Faraday from taking his shot at Myra.

Just then, a single shot cracked in the distance, echoing down the mountain, accompanied by the sound of an angry hornet whipping through the air. The sound ended with a wet, cracking sound of lead digging through Faraday's skull.

At first, the killer looked confused and mildly stunned. His head lolled forward and his hat fell to the ground, exposing the fresh hole that had been blown through his forehead. Next, the pistol slid from his fingers and he dropped to the ground, leaving Danny standing there shaking like a leaf in a stiff breeze.

Clint looked down from the ridge and let out the rest of the breath he'd been holding. The rifle was still smoking in his hands and the shot still echoed in his ears. Once he spotted movement from Rayburn, Danny, and Myra, Clint got to his feet and ran down the trail to retrieve a length of rope from Eclipse's saddle.

Running back to the ridge as fast as he could, Clint was able to get to the remaining shooter as the other man was just beginning to stir. Clint grabbed hold of that man's collar and dragged him toward one of the nearby trees that had the thickest trunk he could find.

Before the shooter had a chance to clear the cobwebs from his brain and get a good look around him, he found that he couldn't move his arms. His hands were similarly restrained as were his legs. When he tried to lean forward, he couldn't move so much as half an inch.

"Hope you had a nice big breakfast," Clint said while

securing the final knot holding the shooter's ropes in place. "Because you're not going anywhere for a while."

After stuffing one of the dead men's scarves into the shooter's mouth, Clint went back to Eclipse, hopped into the saddle, and rode down to the wagon still waiting on the trail below.

THIRTY

Following Clint Adams hadn't been much of a problem. In fact, as he thought back to just how easy it had been Krackow had to wonder if the man he was after really was the Gunsmith after all. From all the stories he'd heard, Clint Adams was supposed to be quick as a flicker and smart as a whip. He was supposed to be indestructible and tricky as a fox.

Smiling to himself as he sat on his horse and rubbed his hands together, Krackow began to wonder what people said about him. Did they tell stories about him in saloons when there wasn't anything else better to do? Or was he just some ghost story left in the wake of the crimes he'd committed? Honestly, he didn't much care what people said about him. In fact, Krackow doubted that that many people even knew he existed . . . which was exactly the way he'd wanted it.

Krackow's gray spotted mare twitched and shuffled on its feet, probably trying to shake off the oppressive cold that soaked into everything in this part of the country. When he'd followed Adams out of Brookins, Krackow's blood had been pumping hard enough to warm his entire body. Now, however, he'd been doing nothing but watching, listening, and waiting.

Watching Adams take out at least four of Malloy's

hired guns on his own, with the others being dispatched by some clumsy boxer with a cowardly heart.

Listening to gunshots crackle through the air, voices raised in the heat of combat, and the woman crying out in fear.

Waiting for the opportunity to pitch his orders to the wind and go join the fray. Waiting for an excuse to take some of the fun for himself.

Krackow had almost charged into the fight to claim some blood for his own, but then he saw that Malloy's men were actually going to lose the confrontation even though they outnumbered Adams and the boxer five to two. In fact, from what he could see from his vantage point, the woman actually played a part in taking down the supposed killers who'd been sent after them all.

At first, Krackow had been disappointed to know that he wasn't the only one put on this job. But now that he'd gotten a look at the others in Malloy's employ, he knew why he'd been contacted.

The fight was over now and Krackow held his position until he saw Adams charge down from the ridge like the soft-hearted hero he was. Krackow waited until he could move without being seen and then touched his heels to his horse's side and headed up to the ridge.

The killer's ears were waiting for any sound of someone approaching, but all they got was voices and footsteps coming from down below. He rode the horse up as far as it could go before hopping off and making his way up the narrow trail. The first thing he spotted was the body of one of Malloy's men, a cocky kid who'd bragged about being one of the deadliest guns this side of the Mississippi River. Looking down at the fellow's dead, blood-soaked corpse, Krackow had to laugh.

"Hope he paid you in advance," he said while bending down to rummage through the dead man's pockets. He found a locket and a small roll of bills. The locket opened up to a picture of a young brunette wearing the confident smile that she had a man she could love. Krackow had seen that smile so many times . . . always in dead men's pockets.

Once again, the killer laughed to himself. He kept the locket and counted the money. There wasn't much, but enough to pay for a hotel and a few more turns with a prostitute he'd come to appreciate in town.

Krackow moved on to the next body, which belonged to another of Malloy's men. This one favored knives and had less money in his pocket than the first. No big surprise there.

Even though he'd seen the man tied to the tree, Krackow decided to ignore him until now. He approached the shooter and looked down at him, waiting for the man to say something or just make any kind of noise. Instead, the shooter had the painfully quiet expression of a man that had had his tongue cut out.

"Did you happen to hurt Adams before he did this to you?" Krackow asked.

The shooter's first reaction was to nod, but he froze and then shook his head instead.

"Is Adams coming back for you?"

The shooter had to swallow a few times and lick his lips before he was able to get out much more than a raspy mumble. "H-he said I wasn't going anywhere for a while."

"Well, at least he was right about something." With that, Krackow snapped his hand forward and jabbed the knife he'd taken off the last body into the shooter's stomach. He didn't stick it in far enough to kill the other man, but instead only pushed the blade in about an inch or so.

Krackow clamped his other hand over the shooter's mouth just in time to catch a scream that would have brought Adams running back with his gun drawn. "No, no, no," Krackow said as he thought about being found by Adams. "Not just yet."

The shooter was wriggling and thrashing about inside his ropes, biting down hard on Krackow's palm. He tried to twist away from the other man, but all he managed to do was tear a bigger hole in his own side. For such an average looking man, Krackow held on to that knife with an iron grip. Even as the shooter kicked his feet and bashed his knees into Krackow's hip, the other man didn't move an inch.

Using the hand that was pressed against the shooter's face, Krackow pushed his victim back until his head pounded against the tree trunk to which he was bound. He did this a few more times, harder every time, until the other man stopped his struggling. Krackow could tell the shooter was about to pass out, so he pulled the knife out until just the tip was inside.

Leaning in closer, Krackow whispered as though he was consoling a child. "Before you ask, I'm doing this to leave a message for Clint Adams. If he finds you before all your blood runs out of this hole I made, tell him that I'm right behind him, watching every little thing he does."

Before Krackow completely removed the knife, he gave it a little twist one way and then the other, savoring the way the shooter convulsed and thrashed inside the ropes.

"And if you don't see him before you die," Krackow continued, "just make sure to go out with a big smile on your face." He turned the knife so that its tip was pressed against a soft bit of flesh just beneath the skin and then stuck it into that flesh with a short, quick jab. "Yeah," he said as the shooter's face twisted into a painful, agonized mask. "Just like that."

THIRTY-ONE

After making sure that Rayburn and his family were all unharmed, Clint hopped back onto Eclipse and scouted ahead to make sure that Malloy hadn't planned any other surprises for them. Although he only checked about a mile ahead, Clint was fairly certain that the men they'd encountered were probably the only ones that had been sent after them. At least, for the time being anyway.

Clint circled back and then returned to the wagon. Once he got there, he saw Myra sitting in the back, holding her son and rocking back and forth. Rayburn had gotten them moving and seemed eager to put the carnage behind him. Danny didn't say a word when he came by and all he got from Myra was a nod and a halfhearted smile. He then rode up to the front and came alongside Rayburn.

"Did you get hurt back there?" Clint asked.

Rayburn shrugged and snapped the reins. "Nah. I'm doing all right."

"Is that blood on your leg?"

Shifting in his seat, the fighter made an effort not to look at his wounded thigh. "It could've been a lot worse."

"Well, it might just get a lot worse if you don't take care of it. Even a little nick can turn into gangrene and then you'll be without a leg. Wouldn't make it through too many fights that way."

"Myra patched me up after you went to scout ahead. It hurts, but I'll manage well enough."

"How's she and the boy doing?"

That question seemed to affect Rayburn even more than the bullet that had torn through his flesh. Shifting in his seat, the fighter winced and let out a groan. "I nearly caught another one back there. Took a piece outta my back." Once he'd found a better position, Rayburn said, "She thinks I'm a coward."

"Did she say that?"

"No, but I can tell." Rayburn grit his teeth and cursed under his breath as though some amateur had snuck in a sucker punch. "If she don't think it, then I know I sure as hell do. It's the truth, ain't it?"

Clint let the question hang in the air for a minute or two until it was lost amid the rumble of the wagon wheels and the slow plod of the horses. Finally, he turned back to Rayburn and asked, "Do you know how to use a gun?"

"It don't take a genius to pull a trigger." Suddenly, the boxer cut himself off and looked over to Clint as though he'd been scorned. "No offense meant."

Clint shook off the apology. "Then maybe I should ask a different question. Have you ever killed a man?"

"No, but that ain't the point. When someone threatens a man's family, he should be ready to do—"

"He should be ready to do whatever he has to do to keep them alive," Clint finished. "And you know just as well as I that if you'd have moved so much as an eyelash the wrong way, Danny would have been dead. Myra too, probably."

Although Rayburn didn't seem ready to argue with Clint, he didn't seem all that pleased with his either.

"Who was that Indian I saw back there?" Clint asked.

A dark cloud seemed to settle over Rayburn's face just then. He lowered his eyes and shifted his feet, ignoring the pain that those movements caused. "I don't rightly know."

"He didn't look like he was in very good shape. Did Myra do that too?"

From out of nowhere, laughter bubbled up from the back of Rayburn's throat and spilled out of him, shaking his muscular shoulders and rocking the driver's seat upon its rusted springs. "All right, Mister Adams. I see what you're saying. You've done yer part."

"We've all done our part, Eddie. And please . . . call me Clint."

The uncomfortable laughter ran its course, leaving Rayburn a little better than before he'd started talking. Looking up to the sun's position in the sky, Rayburn pushed the team a little harder to try to make up for some of the time they'd lost.

"You still got that gun?" Clint asked.

Rayburn patted his jacket pocket. "Don't think I'll be doing much without it for a while."

"Good, because I want to double back and make sure we're not being followed. If you spot something that even looks like it could be trouble, you shoot that gun into the air and I'll head back."

For a moment, Rayburn looked as though he was about to refuse Clint's proposal. Out of sheer pride, the fighter seriously considered taking on whatever was ahead of them on his own. If only to prove his worth to himself, he found himself hoping to run into trouble while Clint was gone, just so he could handle it on his own. But then he thought about the cold, harsh reality of what he'd gotten himself and his family into. They sure didn't need any more troubles.

"Sure, Clint. And thanks again. You better be thinking of a way for me to pay you back for all you done, because I don't take charity from anyone."

Clint nodded and turned Eclipse until the Darley Arabian was facing the opposite direction from the old wagon. With a touch of Clint's heels upon its side, the stallion bolted back toward the ridge.

THIRTY-TWO

As soon as he turned up the narrow trail, which led up to the ridge where he'd found the shooters, Clint could tell that someone else had been there since he'd left. After dodging bullets, knives, and fists in those bushes, he'd damn near committed them to memory. Besides that, whoever had been there didn't seem too concerned about covering their steps.

There were fresh tracks laying over the ones he'd left behind. After dismounting and jogging up to the small clearing, Clint saw that the bodies of the men he'd killed had been moved. What looked like the contents of their pockets lay strewn about the ground as though it had been picked through by scavengers. When he saw the man that had been tied to a tree, Clint ran forward, searching for any sign that he wasn't alone.

Drawing his gun just to be ready for an ambush, Clint searched the area as quick as he could before getting to the shooter's side. "Who did this to you?" Clint asked as he examined the horrific wound in the other man's side.

The bloody gash looked as though someone had simply torn through the flesh and tried to make as big a hole as they could. There was so much blood on the man's clothes and flowing down his body that it formed a dark, stagnant pool on the ground that steamed as hot gore dripped onto cold dirt.

The shooter's skin was pale as the snow-covered bushes, which gave Clint the sudden impression that he was trying to talk to a ghost. Still, he crouched down and fished a folding knife from his pocket, which he used to cut the ropes. Although the shooter's eyes were open, he was staring off into oblivion without giving so much as a blink.

Clint lowered him to the ground and stared into those wide, unblinking eyes. "Are you still in there?" he asked, not really expecting an answer.

When the shooter twitched and tried to speak, Clint nearly jumped back into the bushes out of pure shock. The pale figure croaked loudly in an attempt to speak. All he got out were horrible, almost animal sounds.

"What happened?" Clint asked after kneeling next to him and propping the shooter's head on his knees. "Were you shot?"

After a few more attempts, the sounds coming from the shooter started sounding less like random grunts and more like syllables. "K-Kra . . ."

Clint could tell that the shooter wasn't going to be able to say much of anything else. "It's all right. Don't waste your breath. You probably don't have much of it left anyway."

". . . find you . . ."

"What was that?"

Choking back the waves of nausea and pain that flowed through his body, the shooter swallowed hard and fought to get the words out. "The . . . one that did this to me. He'll find you."

Clint could feel his hands getting warmer as what little blood was left inside the shooter's body poured out onto him. "Who are you talking about? Who did this?"

"D-de . . ." Another hard swallow and this time, the

shooter's breath came out in a trickle of blood. Suddenly, his body was wracked by a hacking cough, which shook him like a pair of rough invisible hands. "The devil came for me," he spat out. "And now he's after you."

THIRTY-THREE

Although he knew he should still be on the trail, Krackow couldn't keep himself away from Brookins for one more moment. Actually, he couldn't keep himself away from a certain woman in Brookins who would be only too happy to hear about all the things he'd done to fill this very busy day.

As always, nobody paid much attention to Krackow as he raced toward town and past the few homes and stables on the outskirts. Even as he slowed his pace and said the occasional hello to folks as they crossed his path, the killer still didn't seem to attract more than a passing glance.

All that changed, however, as he pulled his mare to a stop in front of a two-story building marked AGGIE'S PARLOR in big, flowing red letters scrawled across the large picture window. Aggie's was one of the biggest cathouses in town and there were always plenty of men in and around the place. But it wasn't the men who paid Krackow any mind. Instead, it was the women who worked the place that noticed the minute Krackow walked through the front door.

Aggie's never looked crowded, but that was only because the bordello had so many rooms available on both floors. The main room looked like most others in similar places, complete with a small bar, a piano player, and several plush couches and chairs for entertaining guests who weren't quite ready to adjourn to another room. As always, there were some men scattered here and there talking to women in various stages of undress, all too wrapped up in their conversations to notice anything happening farther away than two feet away.

Krackow loved places like these. First of all, bordellos were the perfect place to kill a man without him ever seeing it coming. Whether he was in bed or just trying to sweet-talk a girl who'd already been paid off to powder her nose at the right moment, such men rarely even knew they'd been shot until someone was shoveling the dirt on top of their coffin.

Mostly, however, Krackow drifted into such places because the women there could fully appreciate a man like himself. Whores tended to enjoy being with a man unlike all the unfaithful husbands or randy cowboys they saw day in and day out. They liked the dangerous men and anyone spending more than a few minutes with Lawrence Krackow could tell that he was indeed dangerous.

The killer stopped in the front parlor and took off his coat. After pulling in a deep breath of the fragrant air, he walked past a group of slovenly locals groping women who laughed unconvincingly at their drunken attempts at romance and headed straight to the back of the room.

Watching the movement of the people as they crossed his path and milled about the parlor, Krackow found the girl he was after and fixed her with a gaze that he saved only for times when he wanted to be noticed. The effect, as always, was immediate. As soon as he changed his bearing, the girl looked away from the man who'd been talking to her and looked straight at Krackow.

Giselle was a slender girl in her early twenties with sandy blonde hair piled on top of her head and held in place with a satin ribbon. Her European features made her face look finely sculpted and a little frail, almost like a doll that wasn't meant to be played with. That alone allowed her to charge more than most of the other girls, since she could play up to the image she wore just as well as the tight, corseted dress and black satin gloves.

Most men seemed eager to think of her as a delicate princess, even though they knew damn well that she was for sale just like everyone else in the place. She never had to mingle with the crowds as they entered through her door since there were always men who would seek her out. And she never had to explain why her prices were just that little bit higher than the rest. In fact, most customers expected it to be.

Krackow had spotted Giselle the first time he came into this place after his first job for Malloy. After every job, he felt the need to tell a woman all about it and watch their faces as he went over every painful detail. Then, just when they started to get that little trace of fear in their eyes and began shifting uncomfortably on their feet, he would have his way with them and watch as their fear turned into lust.

Every woman was a killer at heart, Krackow knew. Whether they knew it or not, they all had it in them. Sometimes they deserved what Krackow would do to them after he'd gotten tired of their bodies and the way they looked at him when they thought he was asleep. Sometimes they deserved worse.

But this fine little princess in Aggie's was something special. She deserved his full attention.

"Excuse me," Krackow said to the man standing in his place next to the delicate little blonde. "I think you'd prefer someone a little closer to your level. Maybe one of those waiting by the piano?"

The customer seemed unable to take his eyes off of Giselle and when he finally did, he turned and glared at Krackow with a threat in his eyes. "Keep walking, friend, or I'll fix it so you don't walk again."

Knowing full well who Krackow was, Giselle gave the killer a little smile and looked him up and down. She'd seen this many times before, but she never got sick of watching it.

Already, the customer had turned away from Krackow, thinking his words more than enough to scare the other man away. When he felt the hand clamp down on his shoulder and spin him around, his first impulse was to swing his fist at the other man's face. But when he got a good long look at Krackow's eyes, something in the back of his mind told him not to make another move.

Besides gripping the customer's shoulder, Krackow made no attempt to defend himself or even move from where he was standing. He'd looked into this one's face. He knew he didn't have anything to worry about. "I said find someone else to talk to," Krackow said quietly. "Now . . . leave."

Even though no threat was made and no guns were drawn, the customer felt a chill sweep down his spine as if the hand on his shoulder was carved out of ice. Without another word, he turned away from Giselle and walked away. Quickly.

"You scared him," Giselle said once Krackow had sidled up next to her. "You always make it look so easy."

The killer reached for a bottle of wine sitting on a nearby table and poured some into a tall glass. "It is easy. Especially since all most people know how to do is talk."

"I know you like to talk." Still nursing her own glass of wine, Giselle leaned in close to Krackow until her body was just brushing up against his.

"You're right. But I know how to do a whole lot more than that."

"I know. But first I want to hear about what you've been doing since we last saw each other."

Giselle was a rare breed of women. Unlike most others, she didn't seem at all uncomfortable when he'd told her what he did for a living. In fact, the first time he'd slept with her, she'd been the one asking all about what it was like to do the things he'd done. She asked over drinks, while she'd bathed him, and even while he was on top of her. Not once did she seem even a little bit frightened. In fact, the one time he'd tried to test her resolve by bringing him a trophy from his last kill, she'd spent the entire night with him and him alone. No charge, of course.

"Did you bring me anything?" she asked coyly.

Krackow dug into his coat pocket with a smirk playing across his lips. "Now where did I put that?" he said while slowly sifting through his things. Finally, his eyes lit up and he pulled his hand out so she could see it. Wrapped around his fist and laced between his fingers was a tarnished gold chain. When he opened his hand, Krackow revealed a small locket.

"Awww," Giselle said as she brushed her hands across the chain. "Is this for me?"

"Of course it is."

Her fingertip lingered over one space in particular where something that looked like a patch of rust stained the front of the locket. She touched the patch and felt some of the stuff flake off. Then, after seeing the look on Krackow's face, she knew that wasn't rust staining the metal. "Anyone I knew?" she asked as her cheeks flushed with excitement.

"Possibly." Krackow thought back to when he'd taken the locket from the dead man on the mountain ridge. He fancied that he could still hear the man's last breaths as he reached out to put the locket around Giselle's neck. "Does it matter?"

Caressing the tainted metal, Giselle shook her head and batted her eyelashes. "All that matters is that it came from you. I love it."

"Then why don't you show me how much." Taking her hand, Krackow led her toward the carpeted stairs at the back of the room.

THIRTY-FOUR

Giselle's room was one of the bigger one's in Aggie's. With the money she pulled in from her selected clients, she could nearly afford to buy out the entire place. Instead, she settled on the master bedroom, which was where she took Krackow as soon as they climbed the stairs.

Inside, the bedroom was lush and full of expensive rugs, a silk divider, a mahogany wardrobe, and her own claw-footed bathtub. A small fireplace was situated on the wall opposite her lavish antique bed and as Krackow started to work on a pile of kindling, Giselle made arrangements to have the bathtub filled with hot water.

Soon, one of Aggie's workers was making trips in and out of the room, dumping bucket after bucket of hot water into the tub. While this went on, Giselle sat with Krackow as he told her every last detail about how he'd killed Kyle and the shooter back on the mountain ridge. As he spoke, she fondled the locket and rubbed the flecks of blood against her soft, fragrant skin.

When the bath had been drawn, Giselle stood and pulled at the strings that kept her dress wound tightly around her body. The material loosened its grip around her breasts and fell down to expose her small, supple curves and hard pink nipples. With a slight wriggling motion, Giselle eased the dress down farther until it was gathered around her waist. Her firm stomach trembled with every breath as she closed her eyes and ran her hands down along her skin, tracing between her breasts and then easing down beneath her clothing.

Krackow watched from where he was sitting beside the fire. His back was propped against the base of a small dresser and his shirt lay unbuttoned all the way down to his midsection. He could feel the hardness in his groin, but somehow managed to keep himself from jumping to his feet just to be closer to her.

Turning her back to him, Giselle placed her hands at the edge of her dress, where it gathered above her hips. Slowly easing her hands down, she moved her hips back and forth, working her way out of her clothes the way a snake shed its skin. The material fell away from her body and landed in a pile around her ankles, giving Krackow a glorious view of her slender hips and firm buttocks. She had a dancer's body with muscles that writhed beneath her powdered skin and a slow grace that made her movements almost dreamlike.

Unable to wait another second, Krackow stood up and tore the shirt off his back. By the time he crept up behind her, he was naked as well. Krackow reached around and slid his hands around her stomach while pressing his cock up against her tight little backside.

She wanted to turn around and face him, but found herself suddenly unable to move in his strong embrace. His hands felt coarse and brutal as they worked their way up toward her breasts. Reaching behind her to run her fingers through Krackow's hair, Giselle arched her back and pushed her hips back until she could feel the bulge in his pants pressing even harder up against her body. She quickly turned around even though his hands were still tight around her, just so she could look into the killer's face.

His eyes were cold and seething with a violence that coiled just beneath the surface like a serpent that was only seconds away from striking. He seemed angered by the way she moved against his wishes and an almost feral snarl curled his lips. "You only do what I want and only when I tell you to do it."

Giselle felt powerless against him as she felt Krackow's hands tighten around her hips and push her away. "Then I've been bad. Are you going to punish me?" she whispered.

Krackow's manner didn't soften in the slightest. Instead, her grabbed her hips and pulled her toward him so strongly that it forced a gasp from Giselle's lungs.

"I can make you feel better," she said while slowly lowering herself to her knees in front of him. "I can make you feel soooo good."

Quickly, she loosened his pants and pulled them down. With a bob of her head, she fit his penis into her mouth and began sucking on it while raking her nails down over his stomach. She then took his entire shaft into her mouth until his tip was sliding down the back of her throat. Holding her head there, she tightened her lips around him and moaned softly.

Feeling the vibrations in her throat against his rigid pole, Krackow grabbed hold of Giselle's hair and made a fist. When she felt the little bit of pain he caused, she grunted and sucked him even harder. When he let her go, she eased her mouth off of him, running her tongue over his skin as she did.

Now, she followed his lead. Allowing herself to be led back to her feet and over to the bathtub, Giselle watched as Krackow's body moved in the flickering firelight. His motions were sleek and agile and she could only imagine that he walked the same way as he crept up behind his victims and put his hands around their throats. Every time she told him about the men he'd killed, Giselle felt the dampness spreading between her legs. Now, after hearing about two of them, the juices made the lips of her vagina slick and ran down her leg as she climbed inside the tub.

Krackow settled into the hot water and looked up at

the woman standing over him. Giselle's body was tight and trim. When she squatted down on top of him, her breasts fit perfectly inside his mouth. The small nipples grew rigid as they brushed against his tongue and her legs locked tightly around him.

While she savored the way his mouth felt on her skin, she reached back to stroke his cock beneath the water. When she felt his teeth bite down on her, she drew in a quick breath and squeezed him in her fist.

Krackow pushed her back. "Stand up," he commanded.

She did. The water dripped over her skin, but she was too excited to feel the cold bite of the air.

After admiring her for a bit, Krackow said, "Turn around."

She did.

"Now get on your knees."

Gripping the side of the tub with both hands, she got down on her knees and looked over her shoulder. She could see the killer coming up behind her and swore she could already feel his hands upon her. Her pussy was so wet that she could feel her juices dripping down into the water.

"I didn't say you could look at me," Krackow scolded as his hand came down hard on her rump.

Giselle yelped and grabbed the tub harder. A smile came onto her face and she turned away from him. Whipping her hair around and back, she closed her eyes and waited for what she knew was coming next. Just as she'd wanted, Krackow grabbed hold of her hair and pulled it back just hard enough to cause a little pain to mix in with her pleasure. Next, she felt his rigid cock slide between her legs and push up inside of her.

At first, Krackow eased himself all the way inside of her, savoring the hot dampness of her body. He pressed his hips up tight against her tight little backside and ran his hand over the gentle curve of her back. With his other hand still grabbing her by the hair, he pulled her head back and began pounding into her until her delicate facade shattered completely and she was grunting in ecstasy every time his cock slammed into her.

Before too long, she tore herself away from him and pushed him back down into the water. Straddling him, she looked down at the killer and lowered herself down onto him, impaling herself on his hard shaft. She bounced on top of him, moving her hands over her own body and leaning back to feel the waves of pleasure surge through her. Looking down at him, she ran a fingertip along the scars which crossed his chest, imagining the fighters that had put them there and what Krackow had done to them afterwards.

With those images flashing through her mind, Giselle felt the first tickles of her orgasm creeping up from between her legs. Her whole body started to shake and she ground herself against him with all her force.

Krackow watched her as her muscles tensed and her eyes clenched shut. Waiting until the screams started to come from her lips, he stood up and picked her up, out of the water. He held on to her with both hands cupping her bottom and stepped out of the tub. First, he pushed her back against the wall and thrust into her while standing up.

Giselle wrapped her arms tightly around him and felt the pleasure stab through her body. As soon as she started to cry out, she felt herself moving again, this time toward the bed. Once there, Krackow laid her down and climbed on top of her.

He thrust into her again and again, sweat pouring down his chest and his eyes wide open. Krackow didn't want to miss a single second of Giselle's writhing and squirming below him. She stretched her arms out over her head and grabbed hold of the first thing she could find, gripping one of the pillows as though she was about to tear it in half.

Finally, unable to move another muscle, Krackow let out a deep breath as he exploded inside Giselle's body. Once the sensations passed through him, he dropped down on top of her and felt the heat of her body adding to his own.

Something pressed up against his collarbone and when he rolled to the side so he could take a look, he saw the locket he'd given her hanging around Giselle's neck. There was still some traces of blood on the tarnished gold, but not as much as there had been before. Looking down at himself, Krackow saw a few rust-colored flecks sticking to his skin.

"Do you like the present I got for you?" he asked.

Giselle felt for the locket and rested her hand on top of the small piece of jewelry. Lifting it up so she could see better, she opened it and looked at the pictures inside. "Who are they?"

"They're grieving for their dead."

Closing the locket and letting it fall down on top of her naked breast, she reached over to run her fingernails along Krackow's scars. "I love it," she whispered.

Already, the killer could feel his body stiffening and aching to be inside of the woman who smiled back at him.

"And people call me the wicked one," he said, reaching out for her.

THIRTY-FIVE

The rest of the day passed like a pack animal dragging its feet, trying not to freeze solid in the winter wind. Clint hadn't been able to find any more gunmen on their trail and circled back to ride the rest of the way with Rayburn and his family. After a while, the sound of the wheels grinding against the packed earth was enough to put him into a kind of trance where his eyes were focused loosely on the road ahead.

After what had happened with the shooter attack, Myra and Danny kept to themselves in the back of the wagon. Rayburn sat bolt upright in his seat every time he heard so much as a sparrow rustle in some trees nearby. The tension crackled off of him like a static charge.

"You want me to take over at the reins for a while?" Clint asked after the tenth time Rayburn had nearly drawn his pistol on account of a nervous hand.

The fighter scanned the horizon, searching for so much as a shadow that was out of place. "I'm all right, Clint. Just a little jumpy is all."

"A little jumpy? I'll bet if I sneezed loud enough, you'd take a swing at me before you knew what you were doing. Just let me get up there and you can rest a spell."

"I told you I'm fine. Besides, I'd rather have you ready to move in case more of Malloy's killers show up."

Clint had no doubt that they would be seeing more hired guns before reaching Rayburn's cabin in the mountains. However, he figured they wouldn't be making their move until the wagon had stopped for the night. Deciding not to say either of those things to Rayburn just yet, Clint let the fighter be and kept silent for the next several hours.

Rayburn had been right when he'd told Clint about Crown Pass. As soon as they got close enough to see the landmark, Clint knew exactly why it had gotten its name. The trail split several times along the base of the mountains, cutting off into paths that went up into the high ground toward mining camps, hunting lodges, and cabins similar to the one Rayburn owned.

Crown Pass was marked by an outcropping of rocks that sat high above the trail like a small floating island. Growing along the rim of the island was a ring of tree stumps that looked as though their upper halves had been pushed over in a rockslide or possibly an avalanche. The jagged stumps gave the effect of a large crown wedged into the side of the mountain.

"This is it," Rayburn said as he pulled the wagon to a stop.

The sun had dipped below the horizon hours ago, but the group had kept rolling to make up for the time they'd lost earlier in the day. Hopping down from the driver's seat, Rayburn walked a little farther down the path, studying the ground along the edge of the trail. After a few minutes of poking around the bushes, he seemed to focus in on a particular spot and then started clearing some of the bushes away.

"Last time I was here I hid the spot where the trail broke off as best as I could," Rayburn said while picking up a pair of bushes that had just been set on top of the ground. "The trail's not that wide, but we should be able to take the wagon at least halfway up. From there, we'll unhitch the team and load them up with what we need. I can make another trip down in the morning."

Knowing his role, Danny had already climbed from the back of the wagon to sit in the driver's seat. Once Rayburn had cleared a path that was just about as wide as the wagon, Danny flicked the reins and urged the horses forward. It took some coaxing, but eventually the animals fought their instincts and walked on in through the tight-fitting path.

When the wagon was off the main trail, Clint looked back to make sure that there was nobody following them and found Myra standing by herself in the middle of the road.

"I had to jump out before we went in there," she said with a shrug. "Being in that wagon feels cramped enough. I just couldn't bear the thought of riding on that poor excuse for a trail that Eddie found."

Clint rode up next to her and held out his hand. "Would the trip be any easier if you rode with me?"

She took his hand and climbed up onto the back of Eclipse's saddle. "It most certainly would." Wrapping her arms tightly around his midsection, she added, "Oh yes. I like this a lot more."

Once Eclipse stepped onto the smaller trail, Rayburn quickly covered up the entrance with all the branches and pine needles he could find. He and Clint also took large branches in hand and did their best to sweep away their tracks that showed where they'd turned off. Clint had to admit that they'd done a pretty good job of covering up. It wouldn't be enough to fool a talented tracker for long, but then again, a talented tracker wouldn't have much trouble picking up a slow-moving wagon anyway.

Both men waited for a few minutes and surveyed the area. Rayburn then left to lead the wagon while Clint jogged back down the main trail to search for any unwanted tagalongs. Finding none, he went back to the hidden path and hopped back onto Eclipse.

For the next part of the ride, the trail was so narrow that Clint himself was starting to feel the trees closing in on him. Between the dense bushes, the thick stands of pines and the natural width of the trail as it started winding up the side of the mountain, Eclipse had no choice but to stay behind the wagon and keep to the lumbering vehicle's pace. As soon as the trees started thinning out, Clint tried to ride around the wagon and scout ahead, but the edges of the trail were either up against the steep mountainside or dropped off on an icy slope.

Adding to the danger of the trail itself was the fact that the sun had long since gone, which left the moon's pale reflection off the snow to light their way. That might have been enough if not for the fact that the large pines towering over them blocked all but a trickle of the moon's light to filter down to help the riders along their way.

The small caravan rode through the night for another couple of hours that seemed to drag on for what seemed like days. With every minute that passed without the sun shining down on them, the wind got that much colder and sank its teeth into everyone's flesh that much deeper. Even for those used to the bitter cold after living in it for most of their lives, Rayburn and his family were shaking uncontrollably beneath all the coats and blankets they'd piled over their shoulders.

As for Clint, he was just beginning to lose the feeling in his feet and hands when he saw the path widen enough for him to pull up alongside the front of the wagon. He tried to speak, but at first only a jittery mumble would come out. Finally, he was able to form complete words. "Th-this is insane to be r-riding in this c-cold."

"Take a swig of this," Rayburn said as he handed over a flask.

Clint put the container to his lips and was careful not to press too much of the freezing metal to his skin. Tilting it upright, he could feel the welcome heat of fiery whiskey burn down his throat. Normally, he was more of a beer drinker, but this time the whiskey tasted like a gift from above as it warmed his insides while running through his system.

"Obliged," Clint said as he handed the flask back to Rayburn. "But we can't travel much longer in th-this cold."

"Won't have to." Lifting his hand to point up the trail, Rayburn indicated a small post set into the soil about twenty yards ahead. "There's a clearing up there behind that post. It's big enough for the wagon and it's far enough up the mountain that nobody taking the main trail will spot a fire."

"Thank god." Just the mere mention of a fire made Clint feel somewhat better. "I've got about another twenty minutes before parts of me start falling off."

By the time they pulled into the clearing off the side of the trail, Rayburn's flask was empty and both men were starting to feel numb inside as well as out. Even Myra had taken her share of the firewater and was keeping her body pressed tightly against Clint. Danny had fallen asleep under a bundle of most of the blankets, leaving only his nose and part of his face exposed to the elements.

Once a fire was started, Clint felt instantly better. They all gathered around the flames and, for a few minutes anyway, forgot about the long journey that still lay ahead. Once Rayburn and his family were bundled up and sleeping, Clint was keeping watch.

All of his senses were on full alert and even the whiskey's effect had long since burned out of him. He knew he needed to stay sharp until daylight if necessary.

If anyone was coming, it would be during the night.

So Clint sat up in the windy darkness and bone-chilling cold . . . and waited for them.

THIRTY-SIX

Clint kept his blood flowing by getting up and stalking around the area, getting a feel for the lay of the land. While looking out for gunmen or trackers closing in on their position, Clint familiarized himself with the trail they would be taking in the morning and the kind of terrain they would be dealing with.

He was no stranger to survival in the mountains, but Clint was no expert in that field either. He could hold his own when he needed to, but with only a rickety old wagon, and a single family, there wasn't a whole lot of options in case something went wrong in the high country.

That was why wagon trains heading over the mountains were as long as possible. That way there was plenty of other folks to pick up slack from fallen members of the group or to replace equipment or animals that got lost during the trip. According to Rayburn, the trip shouldn't be too much longer, but it didn't take much to end up dead in the frozen wilderness. Especially when there were other men out there more than eager to help make bad odds even worse.

Clint shoved his hands a little deeper into his pockets and stomped his feet into the snowy turf. Maybe it was the cold that was making him feel so paranoid and hopeless. He had plenty of other reasons to be paranoid, but hopeless? No, that one was probably due to the cold.

The wind blew like a hollow shriek between the trees and down the mountainside. Clint felt as though it was a giant hand wrapping around him and squeezing tight until even the marrow inside his bones was turning cold. Besides the howl of the wind, there was another sound.

Footsteps.

He'd heard them coming for a while now, but he was pretty sure he knew who they belonged to.

"Are you doing all right?" came a voice from behind Clint.

Without turning around, Clint said, "Hello Myra. You shouldn't be out here this late."

She sat down next to him on a fallen log and snuggled in close. "Neither should you. Wouldn't it be better by the fire?"

"If someone's trying to sneak up on us, I'll see them a lot better out here."

"You won't see much of anything if you freeze to death."

Clint adjusted his posture and realized he'd lost most of the feeling in his legs. When he wiggled his toes inside his boots, all he could feel was the occasional pinprick of pain. "Actually, I think you may have a point there."

"Let me help you," she said while pulling Clint to his feet and walking with him back to the fire. Once there, she sat with him and watched as he held his hands near the flames and pushed his feet up close to the burning wood.

Clint felt better the moment he got within the circle of light given off by the campfire. It wasn't very big, but the fire was enough to bring the feeling back into his fingertips and feet.

"That better?" Myra asked.

"Yeah. But I shouldn't stay here too long. I need to get back out there so I can keep up my watch."

"Do you really think any of Malloy's men will come back in this cold?"

Clint didn't want to panic her, but he also didn't want to lie. So instead of saying anything misleading, he kept his silence and stared into the flames.

"You think they'll be back, don't you?" she asked.

"I haven't seen anyone after us since we took care of those others. But I don't think that if someone wants Eddie dead that badly that they'd give up so easily."

Myra wrapped her arms around herself and leaned her head on Clint's shoulder. For the next few minutes, they sat and watched as the flames fought against the chilling night wind. After a while, she looked at him, leaned in closer, and kissed him on the cheek. When he turned to look at her, they kissed again, passionately this time, and they didn't move apart until they needed to catch their breath.

"What happened before," Myra said. "In town, I mean. That wasn't something that I do with a lot of men. Actually, I haven't done anything like that since before Danny's father died."

Clint smiled at her, admiring the way her skin glowed in the firelight. Her soft blonde hair shimmered invitingly. "I've been thinking about that myself. I sure wouldn't mind being back in that bed instead of out here."

Myra glanced over her shoulder, checking on her brother and son. Dawn would be arriving shortly and the others hadn't stirred from where they'd fallen asleep. They were both inside the wagon and all that could be heard from that direction was the sound of Rayburn's loud snoring.

Reaching up to hold Clint's face in her hands, Myra kissed him again with all the passion that had coursed through her body on the night they'd spent together. Her tongue gently ran along his upper lip and then slid into his mouth. Her hands began roaming down his body and massaging his muscles, eventually working their way down to his lap where she cupped him through his jeans.

Clint hadn't been so warm since he'd left town. As she caressed his body, Myra stirred a heat inside of him that was like a little taste of summer. His hands reached out for her as well, slipping beneath her jacket to cup her breasts. Even through the layers of clothing, he could feel her warm, supple body responding to his touch. She moaned softly into his mouth as he moved his hand between her legs and rubbed the moist, sensitive flesh beneath her skirts.

"We'll get through this," she whispered into his ear as she nibbled his neck. "I know we'll make it through this just fine because you're here to protect us."

Clint moved his hands up to hold Myra's and he held his face close to hers. Looking directly into her eyes, he said, "Don't worry. I'm not about to let anything happen to you or your family. You'll get to that cabin and then you can start a new life. Maybe in another town after things die down with Malloy."

Because he was so close to her, Clint could see the first hint of a tear forming in the corner of Myra's eye. It looked like a tiny crystal forming at the edge of a lake. It glittered in the moonlight like a diamond and hung in place for a few seconds before breaking loose and trickling down her cheek.

"Malloy won't let us go," she said. "He'll keep coming until Eddie's dead, just to prove that he can do whatever he wants to whoever he wants."

Clint reached up and brushed away the tear with the tip of his finger. "I know. But I also know how to deal with men like that. Malloy's nothing special. Just another coward who needs to hide behind a bunch of thugs to prove he's a man."

No more tears came from Myra's eyes. In fact, she seemed to will them back after taking a slow, steady breath. She leaned her head on his shoulder and wrapped her arms around Clint's torso beneath his jacket.

THIRTY-SEVEN

They sat there for a few more minutes, holding each other and watching the fire. Suddenly, Myra got up and pulled Clint to his feet.

"Wait here," she said. Then she went to the wagon and returned with an armful of blankets. As soon as she was next to Clint again, she wrapped several blankets around them both and started walking for the trees on the outer edge of the fire's light.

They were in a small clearing separated by the fire only by a few trees, which were just thick enough to separate one area from the next. Only because there was a fire going was Clint able to see through the branches and to the campsite. When he'd been approaching the smaller clearing, the area looked like just another dark spot along the side of the trail.

After leading Clint into the smaller clearing, she laid out a thick quilt onto the ground and lowered them both onto it. She then threw the other blankets on top of them both and snuggled in closer to him. "This is even warmer than it was by the fire," she whispered, her hands roaming freely over his body.

Surprisingly enough, Clint had to admit that the cold was the furthest thing from his mind. He knew what she was doing and Clint wanted to get back to his watch, but the more she touched him, the more he wanted to touch her. Soon, they were peeling off layers of clothing while struggling to stay under the blankets. Every so often, the blankets would fall off of them and they would get a gust of cold air over their skin. Unlike before, the breeze felt more exhilarating than chilling and only made. Clint appreciate just how warm Myra truly was.

"I don't think this is a good idea," Clint said, even as his hands continued to search for the next hook to pull free or the next button to unfasten.

Myra shrugged free of her dress and slid her arms beneath Clint's shirt. Her clothing was just another blanket loosely wrapped around her now and Clint was wearing nothing but his jeans beneath the cocoon-like bundle.

Her hands rubbed down his chest and pulled his jeans halfway off. "I need you right now, Clint. If anyone's out there, you'll hear them coming. Besides, we're hidden better than before now."

Clint wrestled with what he wanted to do and what he knew he should do. As Myra worked his pants all the way off, however, what she said began to make a lot of sense. Besides, his body needed to warm up for a while and since it looked like he would be the only one keeping watch, he needed to refresh himself for the next day. And at the moment, Clint couldn't think of any better way.

"We'll have to keep quiet," he said as he felt through the layers of discarded clothing to find Myra's naked body tucked away in the middle of it all.

She climbed on top of him and straddled his hips, keeping her body low and close to his. "That's going to be half the fun."

The first thing Clint noticed as Myra got on top of him was how warm her body was. Even though he'd been warming up himself as they'd crawled beneath the blankets, her skin seemed as if it had just been pulled out of a fire. Her breasts pressed up against him and when she wrapped her arms around him, Clint felt her hold him so tight that it nearly took his breath away.

Already, Myra wanted to let out a contented moan. With her legs on either side of him, she reached down and guided Clint between her legs until his hard shaft slid inside her body. As she lowered herself down and took him all the way in, she had to bite down on her bottom lip to keep from crying out with pleasure.

Clint's hands roamed over her strong back, feeling the muscles move as she worked back and forth, up and down on top of him. Her rounded backside fit perfectly into his hands and when she took a moment to catch her breath, Clint began pumping up into her.

This time, she did give out a little squeal. And as he thrust harder, she leaned down and pressed her face against Clint's neck so that what little noise she couldn't control was muffled by his flesh.

They moved as one. Writhing beneath the blankets, Clint and Myra savored each other's bodies until she no longer had the energy to remain on top of him. The blankets slid off of them just a bit as Clint rolled Myra onto her side. The cold air slid beneath the blankets and along their skin like invisible fingers reaching out to give them another sensation to enjoy together.

Myra was breathing heavily as Clint settled in behind her. They were both laying on their sides and as soon as Clint ran his hand along the edge of her thigh, Myra lifted her leg up and back, allowing him to enter her from behind. Since she had nothing else to hold on to, Myra grabbed hold of the blankets and wrapped them tightly around her, moaning into the layers of material every time Clint pushed deep inside of her.

Reaching around to cup her full, rounded breasts, Clint thrust his hips forward and felt his hard shaft glide easily between her legs. He kissed Myra's neck as he continued thrusting, biting occasionally as if he was testing her limits before she could no longer keep herself from screaming out loud.

As the pleasure started overtaking them both, Clint pounded harder, thrusting deep inside as Myra wriggled against him. At the last minute, Myra spread her leg open wider and hooked it around Clint, allowing him to penetrate just a little deeper. As he buried himself between her legs, she twisted around so she could kiss him deeply on the mouth.

Their passion swept through their bodies, causing Myra to moan loudly as her tongue slid past his lips. The more she tried to hold it back, the more she sounded as though she was growling after each and every thrust. When she reached her climax, Myra arched her back and clawed at the ground. Clint, too, felt the explosion welling up within him and he thrust into her one last time before every nerve in his body fired off at once.

They held each other for a few minutes, feeling the way the winter breeze brushed over their faces. As much as he'd hated to do it, Clint slipped back into his clothes. He couldn't get himself to leave the warmth of those blankets however, or the soothing touch of the woman who shared them with him.

"I never thought this would be possible," she said, breaking the utter stillness of the night.

"Thought what would be possible?"

"That I could feel this good so soon after all that's happened. I know it won't last long, but I'll enjoy it for as long as I can."

"I guess that's all anyone can do," Clint said.

Suddenly, a sound from farther down the trail caught Clint's attention. His ears perked up and his hand instinctively went for his gun. His heart skipped a beat when he didn't find the modified Colt at his hip, but then he remembered setting the gun belt next to the blankets as he'd gotten undressed.

"What's the matter?" Myra asked, sensing the tension that had gripped every one of Clint's muscles.

He spoke just loud enough for her to hear. His eyes never once stopped searching the land around them. "When I say, you run for the wagon and don't stop until you get there. No matter what you hear, understand?"

"But Clint, I—"

"No," he said while quietly strapping the gun around his waist. "Just go. *Now*."

THIRTY-EIGHT

All Clint heard was the rustle of a branch and the subtle snap of a dry twig. Any other time or place and he might not have paid the sounds any mind. But after having spent the last several hours listening to every sound that this part of the mountain had to offer, Clint knew that those two sounds did not belong.

With most of the leaves either frozen to the ground or long since blown away, there wasn't much left to rustle in the breezes. And there didn't seem to be much game this far away from the thicker forests higher up the mountainside.

But more than that, it was something in his gut that made him go for his gun. And when he jumped to his feet, he kept his back to Myra, watching out for anyone coming in her direction as she bolted out of the blankets and ran straight for the wagon. The moment Clint heard that she'd reached the wagon, he ducked down low and sought what little cover there was behind the dense bushes.

The next sound he heard was definitely a footstep. Whoever was approaching must have known he'd been found out and was no longer even trying to sneak up on the campsite. Clint looked in the direction that the sounds were coming from and saw nothing but darkness. At times, the noises seemed to be coming from different directions, but that could just as well have been due to the open air and swirling winds.

Backing up toward the wagon, Clint was fairly sure that the steps were only coming from one direction and he faced that way as he moved.

Just then, a figure separated from the pitch blackness outside the campsite. It looked like a single person moving toward him with his hands raised high in the air. After focusing on that figure, Clint could pick out three more farther behind the first.

"Stop right where you are," Clint said to the figure.

Whoever it was, he did as he was told and kept his hands above his head.

Ducking back so that he was away from the dying firelight, Clint stepped into the shadows so that he would be just as hard to see as the newcomers were to him. Rayburn had done a good job of picking the spot, since there was only one way to get to it that wasn't choked off by thick, gnarled bushes. If anyone was trying to come up on the site from any other direction besides that one, which Clint was watching, they would either be sliding down the mountainside or making so much noise making their way through the bushes that they would have been heard for miles around.

Satisfied that he wasn't about to get flanked, Clint turned all of his attention back to the figures making their way down the trail. With his hand on his gun and his body ready to spring into action at any given moment, Clint looked around the edge of his cover.

"What do you fellas want?" he asked.

"Just to talk, Mister Adams."

Clint recognized the voice. He'd heard it not too long ago, although it seemed like it had been ages since he'd been back to Brookins.

"What the hell do you want, Malloy?"

The short, balding man took another few steps closer to Clint and like the ever obedient shadow, Jorgenson was just a few more steps behind. Malloy wore his normal smug expression, which Clint didn't need proper lighting to see.

"Mind if I share your fire?" Malloy asked. "Or would you rather have me and my associates freeze to death?"

"Seems like that would save everyone a whole lot of trouble."

"Then why don't I make this brief. You've chosen to pick sides in a fight that isn't yours, Mister Adams. You got caught in a crossfire, and for that I am truly sorry. I had no intention of getting anyone else involved with my affairs. But since you've become wrapped up in them anyway, I'm allowing you this opportunity to back out. No harm done."

"No harm, huh? I guess those were the orders you gave to the men that ambushed this family earlier today. And those were the orders you gave to the man who held a gun to that boy's head. Am I right?"

Malloy listened to Clint speak with his arms crossed over his chest. Jorgenson shifted on his feet as though he would have rather been in a cave with a hungry wolf pack than where he was at that particular moment. The rest of Malloy's group stayed back in the deeper shadows. They'd moved in a little closer as the moments ticked by, but one of them held back. That one stayed put, frozen to the ground like one of the frosted pines.

"You made me an offer when you first came to town," Malloy said. "Or was that just a way to buy time while you smuggled out a man who wasn't much more to you than a complete stranger?"

"That offer expired when you took those shots at me. Besides, I had a feeling that you wouldn't want to take that money."

"You think you know me, Mister Adams?"

"I know your kind well enough. But that doesn't matter, because you've shown your true colors several times since then."

Clint's eyes had become adjusted to the thick blackness

during the exchange, which was why he'd spotted the little signal Malloy gave to the men behind him with a flick of his hand. It wasn't much more than a twitch, but it brought the others up a little closer.

Clint let them step closer. He was ready for them.

THIRTY-NINE

Clint could see the other men behind Malloy well enough to know they were there, but not well enough to know when they were about to make their moves. Rather than start the fight now, since surely one was coming, he decided to prepare himself just a little bit more. He wanted to bring them in closer.

"How'd you find us?" Clint asked.

Malloy laughed once under his breath. It sounded like a pig snorting with its nose buried deep in a pile of wet mush. "Kyle was loyal enough to Rayburn in his own way, but he was a far cry from a smart man. All I had to do was let that fool talk long enough when he was bragging about how he'd defied me by winning that two-bit fight of his. He told me Rayburn was planning a getaway. I've had men following him ever since then."

Using the time that Malloy was flapping his gums, Clint had moved himself close enough to Malloy so that he could see the men behind him. He couldn't see the looks in their eyes, but he could see their hands well enough. He would know when they went for their guns. And he would beat them to the draw.

"So you found us," Clint said. "Now what?"

"Now . . . you get one more chance to be reasonable

and let me extract my payment for being wronged by
Mister Rayburn."

"You know I can't allow that."

"Then I'll have to take them . . . as the old saying
goes . . . over your dead body."

Clint saw the man directly behind Malloy move for his
gun, which gave him plenty of time to draw his Colt before the other man cleared leather. Malloy turned and
ducked his head as the gunshots started exploding through
the air. The first one to fire was Clint, who sent a round
into the first gunman's chest and through his lung.

Malloy's hired hand fought to bring his gun up and
return fire, but he only made it halfway before the pain
from his fresh wound caught up to him and dropped him
to his knees. His finger squeezed on the trigger more out
of shock than anything else, shooting the bullet wide and
into the bushes.

Once the fight had started, Clint's eyes took in everything even clearer than before the guns had went off. As
the adrenaline rushed through his body, it seemed to
sharpen his senses as well, giving him the advantage that
made the difference between common men with guns and
those of legend.

He watched as the man he'd shot dropped to his knees,
and immediately searched out the next one that was a
threat. The man closest to Malloy was a tall scarecrow of
a man who seemed as though he was only going for his
gun to keep on his boss's good side. And farthest away,
still standing shrouded in darkness, was a man of average
height and build who wasn't moving a muscle.

"What the hell's going on?" came Rayburn's voice
from behind Clint.

Clint didn't take his eyes off the men in front of him
and merely said, "Malloy's here and he brought friends
with him."

"Well that's good," Rayburn said. "Because I brought
some friends of my own."

Out of the corner of his eye, Clint saw Rayburn step

up beside him. He also saw the stout barrel of a shotgun. Bullets whipped through the air as Malloy's gunmen fired off their first rounds and Clint felt a massive hand shove him toward the bushes. When he turned for a better look, he saw that Rayburn not only had the shotgun in one hand, but the small pistol he'd taken from the Indian in the other.

Before he could warn the fighter, Clint saw the wounded gunman raising his pistol, using both hands to take another shot. With one quick motion, Clint snapped his gun up and fired, aiming as though he was pointing his finger at the other man. The gunman jerked back and dropped to the frozen ground like a sack of rocks. His pistol barked once in his hand and Rayburn grunted next to him.

"Are you hit?" Clint asked.

If Rayburn answered, the words weren't loud enough to make it through the twin explosions that came when Rayburn pulled the triggers of both guns in his hands. Gripping the pistol in his left hand, Rayburn fired at the skinny man next to Malloy. He held the shotgun in his right hand, which was just strong enough to keep its grip around the weapon as it bucked inside his fist. Any other man wouldn't have been able to hold a shotgun one-handed at all, but Rayburn's claw-like fist easily kept its grip, even as the shotgun exploded like a miniature cannon.

Clint kept his eyes focussed on the thin man next to Malloy, waiting for that one to take his shot. As soon as he saw Rayburn fire at him, Jorgenson turned and aimed at the fighter.

"Hey!" Clint shouted before Jorgenson could pull his trigger.

Malloy's scrawny aide looked over to Clint and his eyes went wide as he took in the sight of Clint facing him down with smoking gun in hand. He panicked and then did the worst thing he could have ever possibly done: he aimed at Clint.

Clint waited for Jorgenson to swing his hand around and even sight down the edge of his gun barrel. All the while, he hoped that Jorgenson would come to his senses and stop what he was doing before it was too late. "You can walk away from this," he warned.

But Jorgenson would have none of it and his arm straightened out as his finger tensed on the trigger.

Clint was ready to give the man a second chance, but he wasn't about to lay down and die for him. Less than half a second before it was too late, Clint aimed and fired. His first shot caught Jorgenson in the shoulder, which Clint had hoped would spin the other man around and get him out of the fight.

Jorgenson did drop, but he managed to keep hold of his gun and wasted no time in bringing it up to take his shot. With Rayburn getting ready to fire again at Malloy, Jorgenson knew he'd be able to put the fighter down before he sent himself and his employer straight to hell. His arm hurt as he moved it, but he knew he had to kill that fighter. When he heard the next gunshot, Jorgenson thought it had come from his own pistol. But then his vision started to fade away and he was unable to support his own weight. It wasn't until his back slammed against the ground that he felt the burning pain in his heart and the blood flowing from the hole that had been blown through his torso.

Making sure that Jorgenson stayed down this time, Clint got ready to put another bullet into the man, but saw that the one he'd sent through his heart had done the job well enough. He looked over and saw Rayburn still beside him, getting ready to let loose one more time with both guns.

"I think I got 'im," Rayburn said as he dropped to one knee. His face twisted into a painful grimace as his weight shifted onto his wounded leg.

FORTY

Since Malloy was wearing black and cowering in the darkness, Clint couldn't tell if Rayburn's first shots had struck their target. Although it would have been a miracle for the fighter to miss with a shotgun at that range, that didn't mean that Malloy was dead.

Malloy was, however, curled up in a defensive ball with both hands clenched over his head as if he was expecting the sky to fall on him.

"Hold on," Clint said as he put a steadying arm on Rayburn's elbow. "I'll go fetch that bastard and we can bring him in to the law."

Rayburn's hands were shaking with a rage so powerful that it practically floated through the air in hot waves. "But he owns a piece of everything in Brookins."

"Then we'll take him to another town. If he's fixed bets in more than one state, then the federals will probably want to get their hands on him anyway and Malloy isn't big enough to own them."

Rayburn lowered his pistol, but kept the shotgun where it was. "I'll cover you," he snarled. "Go get him before I change my mind."

Before Clint took a step in that direction, he scanned the area, looking for that one figure that had kept away from the others. The last time he'd seen it, that figure was nothing more than a shadowy outline that could just be seen in the darkness. Clint found that figure standing right where he'd left it. "You," he shouted. "Throw down your guns and come over here. It's all over."

The figure didn't move. Didn't even flinch. And from where he was standing, Clint couldn't make out even a hint of the man's face. Even though he was looking straight at him, Clint began to wonder whether or not the shadow was actually a man or just a piece of the landscape.

Every one of Clint's muscles were coiled tight. Holding his gun at hip level, he took a step toward the figure and then planted his feet. One second, the figure looked as though it was backing up as well, but it had only taken half a step back, putting him in a sideways stance preferred by duelists.

"This can go one of two ways," Clint said to Malloy as well as to the man in front of him. "You can walk away or you can be buried in these woods. Either one, it's your choice."

Malloy was still on the ground, groaning and holding himself with both arms wrapped around his body. Holding the shotgun at the ready, Rayburn walked around Clint and went over to the man who'd brought down all this misery.

Clint watched to see if the figure would make a move toward Malloy or Rayburn, but it did no such thing. In fact, for a second, he swore the shadowy man's eyes glinted in the moonlight.

"Dammit, I'm shot," Malloy said as Rayburn tried to move him.

But Clint would not let himself be distracted. Instead he kept his eyes on that man, waiting for him to make the first move. In any other circumstance, he would have kept on waiting until the other man made his mistake. But there were other people in the area that might get hurt if he waited too long. So Clint made the first move.

Slowly, he eased his hand down. "I'm holstering my

gun," Clint said as he slid the Colt into its place on his hip. "Now why don't you throw down yours and we can work this out without any more blood getting spilled."

The movement came almost immediately after Clint spoke. The figure shifted somewhat and then swung its arm out. Clint reflexively went for his gun, but then he heard the sound of something heavy landing on the ground and he stopped before clearing leather. Laying on the dirt halfway between the two men was a black pistol.

Rayburn was kneeling beside Malloy only about five feet from where the gun had landed. Looking up, he said, "I'll get that."

Clint's instincts screamed at him to get Rayburn away from that gun, but before he could say anything to the fighter, the dark figure snapped into motion. The first thing Clint saw was the glint of light off a second gun held in the figure's other hand as it was brought around from behind his back.

"Rayburn, get down!" Clint shouted.

Rayburn hunched down and knelt as low as he could over the pistol.

Without taking his eyes away from the figure for even the time it took to blink, Clint drew and took careful aim so that he'd be sure not to hit Rayburn. Normally, the other man wouldn't have had enough time to thumb back his hammer, but with Rayburn in the way, the figure got more of an advantage than most of those who'd faced Clint in the past.

That advantage gave the man in the shadows an extra quarter of a second.

Unfortunately for him, it still wasn't enough to squeeze his trigger before Clint got off his shot.

For a second, Clint wasn't sure if he'd hit the figure at all. Even though the other man's gun didn't go off, he still wasn't moving much either. Then, just as Clint was about to get ready for another exchange, the figure dropped to its knees and fell over onto the dirt. His gun went off at that point, but only because his finger had jerked on the trigger as death spasms rocked his body.

Clint walked forward, every one of his senses searching the area for any more surprises. Finding none, he went over to the figure and kicked the gun out of its still hand before rolling the body over using the toe of his boot. The man's face didn't look familiar at first, but then it struck a chord in the back of Clint's mind.

He'd seen the man in Brookins somewhere. Probably in Malloy's office or maybe even near the saloon when Kyle had been killed. Still, he couldn't be sure of which it was. Then again, it didn't really matter much anymore.

Dead was dead.

FORTY-ONE

Krackow stood in the shadows, just close enough to the campsite that he could see the flicker of its dying fire. Over the last few minutes, he'd been able to see the flicker of gunshots as well, followed by the booming thunder that rolled through the trees and in the air like angry spirits.

He was supposed to have ridden in by now so he could back up Malloy and the clumsy, half-witted excuses for killers he'd hired. But Krackow wasn't used to working as backup. He'd been hired to hunt down Adams and the boxer on his own and that was how he was going to do it.

Alone.

Besides, it was simply too much fun to watch the Gunsmith at work. Even though he'd tried to give Malloy and his men all the chances in the world to walk away with their lives, Adams had still been able to get the drop on all of them. Even that last gunman's pathetic attempt at a bluff wasn't nearly enough for him to even get the first shot in.

Yes, Clint Adams was impressive. But he had one weakness that could very well be a fatal one: He didn't know when to cut off his dead weight.

Smiling, Krackow checked his rifle and levered in a round. He then started walking slowly down the hidden trail, being careful to blend in with this environment just as easily as he could blend into a crowd. His eyes had adjusted to the darkness long ago and he was able to spot the branches before he disturbed any of them. His eyes watched the ground just before he took his next step, making sure to avoid stepping on anything that would make a noise louder than a subdued breath.

Within a minute, he was closing in on where the wagon had been parked and was moving in around the rickety vehicle. His steps became slower and even more precise as he edged in closer. He bent at the knees and worked his way through the bushes, keeping low enough that the top of his head was well within the branches.

He could hear them talking now and it sounded like the group had a lot more on their minds than looking for him. Judging by the way they moved about, they thought they'd dealt with all of the dangers the night had to offer.

Krackow's smile widened.

Clint worked his way down through the bushes in the direction that Malloy had come. He couldn't see much besides various shades of black and gray shapes since the moon had been lost behind a stream of passing clouds, but he couldn't hear anyone else approaching either. After gathering up all of the guns that were littered on the ground, Clint went back to Rayburn's side.

The fighter was sitting on the back of the wagon with his feet dangling down. Myra tended to him, wrapping a bandage around his midsection and doing her best to be careful as she worked around a bloody hole in his lower ribs. Danny ran back and forth, gathering water or more bandages whenever his mother ordered him to do so. Malloy was leaning against one of the wagon's rear wheels, the front of his shirt speckled with small red dots.

"Is he going to be all right?" Clint asked as he walked up to Rayburn.

Myra shook her head and brushed a stray wisp of hair from her eyes. "I don't know how he manages it, but his luck's still holding up. I'm no doctor, but it looks like the bullet passed through his side and came out the back. It wasn't very deep."

Clint pulled back some of the bandages and took a look for himself. There was a bloody hole in his side, but it looked as though it mostly went through muscle. "That doesn't look so bad. Still, you need to see a doctor." Looking down at Malloy, he asked, "What about him?"

Malloy tried to get up, but only made it halfway before wincing in pain and dropping back down to the ground. "I'm in a lot of pain, goddammit!" he bellowed. "But none of you seem to care too much about that."

"Quit yer howlin'," Rayburn shouted. "As much as I hate to say it, you'll be just fine." He then looked back at Clint and shrugged. "I didn't bring out that shotgun before because it was only loaded with rock salt. You know, just to scare folks away and such. Guess it didn't do much good."

Clint couldn't help but laugh. "Looks like it did plenty of good to me. This way, Malloy gets to see the inside of a jail cell once all this is over. I'll bet he's looking forward to that."

Malloy started to say something, but then held his tongue. Instead, he anxiously looked from side to side, searching the surrounding area for something that he never seemed to find.

"What's the matter, Malloy?" Clint asked. "Waiting for more of your men to come and save you?"

"No, no," Malloy quickly replied. "Just . . . making sure you're not going to put a bullet in my back."

The fat man was obviously lying. Clint's poker-honed instincts told him that much the instant Malloy had opened his mouth. Taking another look around, Clint searched for what Malloy had been looking for. He knew that unless he knew exactly what he was searching for, he would never find it in this inky darkness.

Crouching down to Malloy's level, Clint grabbed hold of the man by the front of his shirt, making sure that he was rough enough to disturb plenty of the shallow wounds caused by the rock salt. "This game of yours is over, Malloy," Clint said as he pulled the fat man off the ground. "You call off whatever dogs you've got left, or I'll just hunt them down myself. And if you make me go hunting, I'll have your hide laying right next to all the others I bring back. Do you understand me?"

Malloy nodded, a look of pure fear playing across his features.

"What were you looking for just now?"

Fighting his way through the oncoming panic, Malloy looked at Clint with watering eyes and spoke with a shaking voice. "He'll keep coming for you, Adams. Even if you kill me, he'll keep after you and this whole family. The only prayer you have of stopping him is if I call him off."

"Then do it."

Malloy was used to fighting battles of wills, except this time it was different. This time, instead of being confident in his power and influence, his wealth or connections, or even the men he had that would kill at his command, his mind was full of very different images. This time, he saw his men getting cut down and falling dead to the ground. He thought of all the plans he'd made to simply punish a few fighters who'd dared act against him and how those plans had turned so bloody and gone so wrong.

Staring deeply into Malloy's eyes, Clint could see the indecision that the other man felt just as easily as he could read the intentions of a bad bluffer. All the arrogance Malloy had had when he'd been in his office was draining out of him through the bloody holes in his shirt. He'd been hurt and he'd watched his men die. Clint knew that if Malloy was going to be rattled, now would be the time it would happen.

"Come on, Malloy," Clint said with focused intensity. "What are you waiting for?"

A gunshot cracked from somewhere nearby, followed by the sound of Myra's pained cries.

A smug grin slid onto Malloy's face. "*That's* what I was waiting for."

FORTY-TWO

"Oh my god," Myra shouted. "No!"

Clint slammed Malloy back to the ground and stepped around to the back of the wagon. Rayburn was still sitting with his feet hanging over the edge, except the expression on his face seemed wrong. The fighter didn't look at Clint and didn't make a move to respond to the gunshot. He didn't even blink.

At first, Clint thought that the fighter had taken another bullet. Then he saw Rayburn try to speak. When he looked in the same direction as everybody else, Clint saw what had inspired the terror that coursed through Myra as well as her brother.

Standing near the edge of the clearing with his arms loaded with guns collected from the area, Danny walked another step toward the wagon and let everything he was carrying fall to the ground. "M-Mom?" the boy rasped as a bloodstain widened on the front of his shirt just below his neck.

Myra started to run for her boy, but Rayburn found his strength and grabbed hold of her arm, all but throwing her back into the wagon. When he dropped from the back of the wagon, Rayburn stumbled as a burst of pain shot through his wounded leg.

Clint knew that whoever had shot Danny was just wait-

179

ing to take a shot at someone else, but he didn't care about
becoming the next target. In fact, as he ran toward the
boy at full speed, Clint hoped that the next shot would
come his way rather than at any of Rayburn's family.

Being careful of the boy's fresh wound, Clint scooped
Danny up into his arms and kept running away from the
bushes. Another shot came from the darkness of where
the trail met the clearing and a bullet whipped toward
Clint's back. The only thing that kept him from getting
hurt was that he was a moving target and turned at just
the right moment.

Rather than plow straight into his lower spine, the bullet
slammed into Clint's hip and sparked off of metal to be
deflected into the surrounding bushes. The impact of the
glancing blow was enough to make Clint falter in his step.
Before he fell to his face, Clint let Danny go and shoved
him toward the wagon.

"Keep running," Clint said as he stumbled for a few
more steps and then eventually fell down.

The ground came up to smash Clint square in the jaw.
His chest landed next, absorbing most of the impact and
nearly driving the wind from Clint's lungs. Reflexively,
he rolled onto his back and started climbing to his feet
while every muscle in his body cried out in painful pro-
test.

Behind him, he could hear Myra crying and calling out
Danny's name. He could hear Rayburn's boots pounding
on the dirt as well and knew the fighter would want to
take a shot at the newest arrival. But Clint knew the
fighter was hurt and didn't belong this close to the firing
line.

"Get back," Clint said to Rayburn. "Make sure Malloy
doesn't pull anything."

When his hand went to his gun, Clint immediately felt
hot metal and scorched leather. Practiced at finding flaws
in weapons with a single glance or a quick once-over,
Clint didn't even have to look to know that his Colt had

taken the bullet that would have torn through his side and taken his legs right out from under him.

Suddenly, as the last echoes of the gunshot were carried away by the frozen winds, another sound could be heard drifting in from the surrounding bushes. It was laughter.

Krackow stepped from his cover with his gun held loosely in hand. The smile on his face was full of bad intentions and his eyes flicked over Clint and the others like a snake deciding which one to bite first. "This has been more fun than I could've ever thought it would be," he said. "I must say, you put on quite a show, Adams."

Clint covered his gun with his hand and readied himself to draw. "Well it's not over yet." His fingers slowly felt where the bullet had struck his pistol, trying to feel for where it had been hit so he could decide whether or not it should be fired. He knew the dangers involved with such a gamble. At best, it might fire without any accuracy. At worst, it could jam or even blow up in his hand.

"Shoot him!" Malloy shouted.

Rayburn swung his fist straight down to pound Malloy in the middle of his face, knocking his head up against the wagon hard enough to make the whole thing rock back. Malloy's head sagged forward and his body went limp.

"Been wanting to do that for a while now," Rayburn said.

Clint knew just from the sound of it that Malloy would be out of it for at least several hours. "That only leaves you," Clint said to the man he faced. "I would've given you the same chance as the others, but that was before you shot Danny."

"So where does that leave me?" Krackow asked.

"You can throw down your guns and we'll take you in, but I'm pretty sure you'll be a mess by the time we get you back to Brookins. At least you'll be alive, though."

Krackow pursed his lips and tapped his foot in mock contemplation. "Hmmmmm. I don't think so. You see, I've got a job to do."

"Just like you did with Kyle?"

A look of mild admiration drifted across the killer's features. "How did you know that was me?"

"Shooting a man from cover with his back to you, firing before anyone knows you're there, shooting a defenseless child, it all sounds like the same style." As he talked, Clint moved his hand over his gun in an effort to get a better idea of how badly it had been hit. Even after all his stalling, he couldn't say for sure what kind of condition the Colt was in. And there was only one way to find out.

"That's the problem with you legend types, Adams. You talk too damn much. I'm used to a more active form of entertainment. Here," Krackow said as he raised his gun and pointed it over Clint's shoulder and toward the wagon where Myra was tending to Danny. "Let me demonstrate."

As he drew the Colt from its blackened holster, Clint adjusted his aim as he got a look at where the side of his gun had been bent inward. He pulled the trigger, expecting that it might very well be the last time he had use of all his fingers before getting them blown off in a misfire.

Krackow had been hoping to provoke such a reaction and his heart swelled when he saw that he was actually getting a chance to draw down against the Gunsmith. Even though face-to-face confrontations truly weren't his style, he'd been aching for this one.

The killer adjusted his aim with a quick turn of his wrist. Even as he did, however, he could see that Clint had already drawn and was about to pull the trigger. A fraction of a second before Krackow could fire, he knew he was going to be too late.

The sound rang through both men's ears like a clap of thunder, even though it was nothing but a dry, metallic *click*.

FORTY-THREE

Krackow knew that Clint had gotten the drop on him. He knew it right down to the core. That was the reason he didn't even bother pulling the trigger. And when he heard the gun's hammer slap against the side of the cylinder, his eyes lit up like the stars over his head.

"Now that's what I call a show," Krackow shouted as he took his time and started lining up his shot.

Clint was about to charge the killer head-on when he heard a voice coming from the direction of the wagon.

"Behind you," Rayburn said.

Clint turned and saw something flying through the air heading straight for him. In one fluid motion, he dropped the modified Colt and snatched what Rayburn had thrown neatly out of the air. The Indian's pistol fit nicely in Clint's hand and by the time he had it pointed at Krackow, he'd thumbed back the hammer and squeezed the trigger.

The bullet hit Krackow in the middle of his chest, jerking the man back a few paces and throwing off his aim as he fired his gun. Another bullet dug a tunnel through his brain, pitching his head straight back and tossing him backward onto the cold ground.

Krackow's legs twitched in his last moments of life, making it look as though he'd landed on a hot skillet.

With one last shudder, his body burned off its last few impulses and then went limp.

"Damn," Clint said as he looked from the pistol in his hand to the one at his feet. "I love that gun."

When daylight finally came, Clint felt as though he'd stumbled into a graveyard. He knew there had been plenty of men who'd gotten killed in the night, but when he saw their bodies all piled up around them like so much kindling, Clint was reminded of the stories he'd heard of the old days after a particularly bad plague had torn through a populated area.

All around, there were signs of battle and death. The snow was tainted by so much blood that it looked like it had been splattered about by wild animals who'd kicked over buckets of the stuff. At least, that was how Clint felt when he saw the sunlight creep over the horizon.

In reality, there wasn't all that much blood or all that many bodies, but there was enough of both to make the clearing look soiled. The bright sunlight should have reflected off of pure white snow amid a crisp breeze. Instead, there was nothing pure to be seen.

Even Danny had been touched by the violence and awoke covered in blood. Granted, the boy's wounds, although they'd been terrible to look at, weren't too bad after they'd been cleaned up a bit. Krackow's bullet had dug a nasty gash in the side of the boy's neck, which had bled something fierce, but was far from life-threatening. And as for Rayburn himself, the fighter appeared to have endless reserves of strength that kept him going no matter how high his injuries piled up.

While he thought back on these things, Clint felt a pair of gentle hands rubbing the muscles in his back. Eventually, those hands slid around his waist in a familiar way, wrapping tightly around him and pulling him close until Clint could smell the welcome aroma of Myra's fragrant hair.

"There's no more of them coming," she said. "You did such a good job in protecting us."

Clint turned around and embraced the blonde with a strength it had taken all night to muster. "I've spent the whole night wondering how come I couldn't have gotten everyone through this without a scratch. I wonder if your family wouldn't have been better without my help? I mean, just because of who I am, I probably made the people come after you that much harder." Looking over to where Danny slept, he added, "Your son almost died because of me."

Suddenly, Myra seemed to lose all of her frailty and gain back every bit of her own strength. She looked up at Clint with a determination that was strong enough to snap Clint out of the mood he'd slipped into over the last several hours. "I won't hear you talk like that for one more instant, do you hear me? If not for you, my brother would have been dead long ago. Same thing with Danny and maybe even me because nobody would have been there to stand in Malloy's way.

"There was no way for you to keep every person Malloy went after alive and untouched because, Gunsmith or not, you're still only one person. You did a lot of good here, Clint. Be proud of yourself. I know I am."

Clint felt as though Myra had looked into his soul and read what he most needed to hear. Just then, the mountain seemed a lot less desolate and the air felt just a little warmer against his skin. "Thank you," he said.

For the next few moments, Clint and Myra simply stood silently holding each other as the sun climbed its way into the eastern sky. When its rays broke through the trees and exploded across the Rockies, they seemed to clear away some of the blood that had been spilt there. Not a lot, but just enough to make the land feel clean again.

"Come on," Clint said finally. "It doesn't look like there's any more of them coming. We need to head back for town."

Within the hour, the rickety old wagon was moving down the trail once again. Although this time, it was headed back for Brookins rather than up the mountain any farther. The trip went a lot faster than the one that had brought them there. Mainly, that was because of the sense of safety that had settled upon them.

Malloy rode in the back of the wagon tied up like a prize calf and still hurting from the single punch Rayburn had landed the night before. All the fat man could do was grumble to himself about the pain he felt from his broken nose.

"The sheriff will see things my way," Malloy said once they reached town. "He's a reasonable man."

With all the care he would show to an old, rolled-up carpet, Rayburn dragged Malloy from the wagon and tossed him onto the back of one of the horses that had been unhitched from the wagon. "That's why you're not going to the sheriff," he said.

"Wh-what do you mean?"

Clint took the reins of the other horse and looped them around Eclipse's saddle horn. "I'm handing you over to some friends of Rayburn's. They'll keep an eye on you until someone can get a U.S. Marshal down here."

Since Malloy didn't have enough energy left in him to put up much of a struggle, he simply squirmed inside his ropes like a giant earthworm. "That marshal will need proof, Adams. And he won't find none of that here or anywhere else, for that matter!"

Clint got up close to the fat man and spoke in a hard-edged voice that cut straight through all of Malloy's bravado. "If I was you, I'd worry less about that marshal and more about the time you're going to spend with the fighters you've been feeding off of for the last several years. If I was to wager a guess, I'd say you should get used to that broken nose you got, because every other part of you will be broken within the first few hours you're with those boxers."

"Y-you can't do this, Adams," Malloy sputtered as naked fear began to show in his eyes. "Those animals will kill me!"

"Maybe. Maybe not. You'll just have to try to appeal to their good natures and hope they show you a little more mercy than you ever showed them."

Those words seemed to hit Malloy even harder than Rayburn's fist. Malloy looked around as townspeople walked by, watching their faces and how they regarded him with a mixture of contempt and downright hatred. There was no fear in their eyes anymore.

No fear and no pity.